"I'm no

She reached up and pushed a strand of hair out of her eyes, but a warm breeze blew it forward again. Josh caught the strand and tucked it behind her ear.

He ducked his head and glanced in her back seat. "I didn't know you had a daughter."

"She's my sister's little girl, but she's staying with me for a few days."

"You're always helping someone out. I used to admire that about you."

"Used to?"

"Still do. You have a big heart, and it's obvious that you care a lot about your family and this town."

He took a step toward her, and she found herself tipping her head back to look into his face. Behind him, a burst of red lights followed by yellow and green flashed in the night sky, accompanied by a loud boom. "You're missing the fireworks," she told him.

He kept his gaze on hers as more fireworks flashed and boomed. "I'm not missing a thing."

Dear Reader,

I love the story of a bad boy looking for redemption. There's something about a redeemed sinner who is looking to make up for his past that draws me in every time.

In this book, Josh Riley returns to his hometown of Thora to take care of his aging father. He's looking for a chance to prove that he's a changed man and thus decides to run for mayor. Little does he know that his opponent is the town sweetheart, Shelby Cuthbert, who is running out of a sense of obligation and responsibility for the town she's lived in her entire life. The fireworks between them go beyond just the election, and they need to decide what is more important: winning the race or finding love. In my mind, love always wins.

I debated who would eventually win the election and wrote several different endings before choosing the one here. I imagine that it was much like that for the voters of Thora in the story. Either one would be a good mayor, but only one could win. I hope you agree with who does.

Come back in the fall for another story with the Cuthberts when Jack faces a future without his best friend, Mel, who is looking for more than friendship. I look forward to seeing you then.

Syndi

HEARTWARMING

The Bad Boy's Redemption

—

Syndi Powell

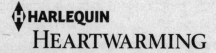

HARLEQUIN®
HEARTWARMING™

ISBN-13: 978-1-335-17983-8

The Bad Boy's Redemption

Copyright © 2021 by Cynthia Powell

Recycling programs
for this product may
not exist in your area.

This edition published by arrangement with Harlequin Books S.A.

For questions and comments about the quality of this book, please contact us at CustomerService@Harlequin.com.

Harlequin Enterprises ULC
22 Adelaide St. West, 40th Floor
Toronto, Ontario M5H 4E3, Canada
www.Harlequin.com

Printed in U.S.A.

Syndi Powell started writing stories when she was young and has made it a lifelong pursuit. She's been reading Harlequin romance novels since she was in her teens and is thrilled to be on the Harlequin team. She loves to connect with readers on Twitter, @syndipowell, or on her Facebook author page, Facebook.com/syndipowellauthor.

Books by Syndi Powell

Harlequin Heartwarming

Visit the Author Profile page
at Harlequin.com for more titles.

This book is dedicated to Josh Groban, whom I've loved since I bought his first album almost twenty years ago. His lyrics inspiring me, I've written each book to the soundtrack of his sultry voice. I often teased my family that he was my boyfriend, which prompted my nephew to insist I ask him to sing at my dad's funeral. Thank you, Josh, for your amazing music!

CHAPTER ONE

BEING THE ONLY candidate currently running for mayor of her Michigan hometown, Shelby Cuthbert was almost guaranteed to be elected.

It was the *almost* part that kept her awake at night.

Pouring her fourth cup of coffee, she debated the merits of checking if another candidate had gathered enough signatures to place their name on the ballot for August's election. She glanced at the time on the punch clock. It was close to three. Only an hour left until the deadline passed.

"Just go, Shelby."

Shelby glanced behind her. Eddie, her chief mechanic and all-around right-hand man in the business, stood stoically next to an ailing Chrysler. "Go where?" she asked.

"City hall. The deadline's coming up, right?"

"You read minds as well as rebuild engines?" She turned back and added cream to her coffee mug and stirred the liquid. "There's no point in me going over there. Besides, I was hoping to scan the internet for that battery lead. I want my car to be ready for the Fourth of July parade."

"Found it online last night, and it'll be here by the end of next week."

"Then I should be going over the books to make sure we're current on our bills paid."

"Which you said you already did this morning."

She peered at Eddie, who had worked at her father's garage for as long as she could remember. She could recall him teaching her the parts of the engine as they rebuilt the one in her Mustang. He'd never treated her like a kid, even though she hadn't been much more than sixteen at the time. She'd worried that being his boss would hurt the relationship they had, but in her nine months of taking over the business, they had never had an issue. Until now. "Are you trying to get rid of me?"

"If you leave early, then there's a chance I'll scoot out and get a nap in before dinner with my wife. Besides, we're caught up for the day."

Eyebrows raised, he watched her patiently. Silently, she debated whether she should go to city hall or not. It wouldn't change anything, so what was the point? "You and the rest of the guys take off. I'll lock up." When Eddie looked at her, she shook her head. "I'm not going down there. Whatever's going to happen will happen, and me being there now won't change it."

"Except it'll give you some peace of mind." Eddie put a hand on her shoulder. "You'd be the best mayor this town has seen, and everyone knows it, so stop worrying about it."

"Thanks, Ed. I appreciate your support."

He nodded and left to tell the other two employees they could leave early. She grabbed her coffee mug and retreated to her office to back up her computer files before leaving for the day.

Business overall was pretty good, but the garage needed steadier work to keep them busy as well as in the black. Ever since her father's retirement, the books told her that things would have to improve or cuts would become necessary. The last decision she wanted to make was to lay off employees who had been loyal to her dad. It'd be tantamount to admitting that she was failing.

Something she'd never do.

Eddie popped into her office. "Everything's put up for the night, and I'm heading out. Stu is coming in at seven tomorrow morning to have his brakes checked, so I'll be in at about six thirty."

"I can open for him."

"It's my job, so I'll do it."

She nodded at Eddie, then turned off her computer. "Go have that nap."

He saluted her. "Have a good night and try not to obsess about the election. You're guaranteed to win."

"There are no guarantees when it comes to politics."

He nodded and left her office. With the employees gone for the day, the garage was too quiet. Figuring an early afternoon exit wouldn't hurt her either, she grabbed her purse and locked the side door before walking to her car.

If she went home now, she'd only be watching the clock every five minutes until the deadline passed. She tucked her car keys back into her purse and strolled down Thora's Main Street to her best friend's bookstore and opened the door.

Melanie Beach looked up from reading what looked like instructions and pushed off the counter. "You're here. Good. I need a second set of hands to help me figure out this machine."

Shelby approached the long, worn counter that held a cash register on one end and housed the coffee bar on the other. Farther back sat a large copper machine with several handles and spouts. "Your new espresso machine came in early."

"This gives me a chance to learn how to operate it so I can teach Emma before the weekend." She thrust the instruction booklet into Shelby's hands. "Read page three to me."

After several attempts, Melanie produced a small cup of espresso that smelled heavenly. Mel took a small sip, then nodded. "Not bad."

She wanted to pass the white demitasse to Shelby, who held up a hand to ward off the cup. "Espresso's not really my thing."

"But coffee is. Just try it."

Giving in to her friend's request, Shelby took the cup and a tentative sip, and frowned. "Ooh, that's strong."

"But not bitter?"

Shelby had another taste and let the flavor linger on her tongue. "No, not bitter." She handed the cup back to Melanie. "So, this is your plan for bringing in more customers?"

"At least until you're mayor and use your brilliant ideas to promote Thora's small businesses." Shelby sighed and claimed a stool. Meanwhile, Melanie frowned at her. "You're still worried about the deadline? Anyone who chooses to run against you would have to be confused, because you're going to win."

Everyone had more confidence in that than she did. "There's no guarantee, even if no one else does enter the race."

"Come on, Shel. You're the town sweetheart. Everybody loves you."

"Not everyone."

"Well, the people who know you do." Melanie took a seat on the stool next to Shelby. "You're smart, compassionate and have the best interests of the town at heart. You want to build the small businesses in town to improve tax revenues. And you have a plan to promote Thora as a busy suburb with a small-town feel to attract more home buyers and business owners. I'm telling you. You're going to win."

"I should hire you to be my campaign manager."

Melanie stuck her hand out. "I accept."

They shook on it, then Shelby hugged her friend. "Thank you. I needed that shot of confidence."

"Why don't you go down to city hall, just to reassure yourself? You know you want to."

"Eddie said the same thing." Shelby smiled. "Fine. I will. You want to get together for dinner after you close tonight?"

"Sure. But we'll have to invite Jack too. We had plans already."

Shelby liked her best friend and cousin hanging out together. She pushed herself off the stool and grabbed her purse. "Well." She took a deep breath. "Here goes nothing."

"Positive thoughts, Shel."

She nodded and exited the bookstore.

Standing on the sidewalk, she opted for the short walk rather than driving to city hall. It was a nice early June day with blue skies and a promise of the warmth that summer would soon bring to Michigan.

At city hall, she glanced at the large clock tower that marked time in Thora. Five minutes to four. Only five minutes and the *almost* part of her election would be removed. She'd be the next mayor of Thora.

She opened one of the heavy oak doors, and a tall man with dark hair ran up from behind and strode past her. He didn't glance back as he sprinted down the hallway. "You're welcome," she called after him.

Muttering to herself about how some people could be so rude, she went to the city clerk's window and paused. The sprinter handed the clerk a stack of papers, and Shelby realized that there were no guarantees, after all.

JOSH RILEY PASSED the pages of signatures required for him to be a candidate for Thora's mayor to the clerk. He'd planned to get the paperwork in much earlier, but getting the required number of signatures had taken him longer than he had expected. True, he might not have been back in town for very long, but this was where he'd been born and raised. People knew him.

Maybe that was the problem. They remembered the juvenile delinquent he'd once been. It had taken him hours and effort to convince folks that time and experience had removed his wayward tendencies and turned him into a strong leader. One who could bring Thora back from near bankruptcy. All he needed was the chance to prove it. In the end, he'd managed to garner just enough last-minute signatures to get his name on the August ballot.

The clerk at the window finished glancing through the paperwork and peered at him. "Everything looks correct." She pointed at the clock on the wall. "You almost missed the deadline."

"Almost, but not quite. I made it before four o'clock, as stated on the petition." He gave her a smile that he hoped charmed her and noted her name tag. "And that's the important part, right, Sandra?"

She gave him a skeptical look, then stamped

each page of signatures before placing the documents into a manila envelope. In turn, she passed him a bright blue folder with the town's coat of arms and its motto, "Suburban city with a small-town heart," printed on the cover. "In there, you'll find the required campaign-finance rules along with a list of election regulations. They're also listed on our town's website if you need further information. In a few weeks, I'll also be contacting you with debate details. The debate'll be held on the Fourth of July, before the annual fireworks. Questions?"

Josh paused. Debate? He'd expected to do some fundraising as well as door-to-door campaigning and kissing a few babies, but an actual debate? He hadn't been in one in years, and even then, he'd relied heavily on his partner to do the legwork while he relied on his humor and quick verbal skills. After all, he'd talked himself out of trouble enough throughout most of his life. He beamed at Sandra. "No questions, but thank you, Sandra. I hope to get the chance to win your vote."

She immediately frowned. "You have no idea who you're running against, do you?"

She shook her head with a low chuckle. "Good luck. You're going to need it."

He placed the folder under his arm and turned, almost crashing into a woman staring at him. Quickly reaching out a hand to steady her, he gazed at her familiar face, but her name escaped his memory. "Are you okay, miss?"

"You're running for mayor?"

He straightened and stuck out his chest. "Proud to. Gotta love the rumor mill if that bit of news is already spreading around town."

"Hmm, it's more the sound waves bouncing off the high ceiling here, creating an echo so that everyone in the building could hear." She continued to stare at him. "You don't really think you can win, do you?"

Why did everyone expect him to lose? He'd been gone long enough that they wouldn't hold his past against him, right? He paused. "Why wouldn't I win?"

The woman looked stunned. "Because you're Josh Riley. The one who spray painted graffiti and obscenities all over the senior rock the week before graduation. The boy who spent more time in detention than he did in class. The kid who the principal thought had broken into the school's computers to tamper with grades. And I haven't even started to mention the broken hearts you left all over town. And you think you can win after that?"

"Okay, okay," he said, lowering his voice. "You've made your point." He grimaced as he recalled all the trouble he'd once gotten into, and that this woman seemed to know so much of it. Hopefully, she'd be the exception. "That was high school stuff. You're not going to hold that against me. I've matured since then, and the voters will recognize that too."

"But you're not a resident. The election rules clearly state that you have to be a resident of Thora in order to be eligible to run for mayor."

"I have been here for the last six months, which my cell phone bills and bank records will show. Or hasn't the rumor mill also shared that I've moved back to take care of my dad?"

The woman opened and closed her mouth several times, clearly flustered by him. Hoping to redeem himself, he held out his hand. "I hope I can earn your trust and gain your support for mayor."

She looked incredulously at his hand as if he'd offered her a dead fish. "You don't remember me, do you?"

He let his hand fall as he racked his brain for her name and landed on one.

A long-forgotten memory of sitting with her in a library surfaced. She'd worn her hair longer then, and it had darkened to auburn from the strawberry blond it had once been. But how could he have not remembered those bright blue eyes? Another memory popped up, and he winced. "Right. Shelby Cuthbert. How could I forget?"

"And yet you did. More than once, if memory serves." She fiddled with her purse strap. "I had heard that you moved back to town after your mom died. I haven't seen you at any of the city council meetings. Maybe if you had been there, I would have discovered before now that you planned on running for political office."

Maybe he should have made more of an effort to have gone to a few of those meetings. "With Mom gone, I've been cooking and caring for my dad. That means most of my evenings are spent at home with him and not going to meetings."

"And how does Bert like having you back in town? Pleased, I'm sure." The way she asked the question made it apparent that she didn't know everything about him. His own dad had refused to sign the petition. It had been an old friend of his who'd convinced him that running for mayor would be the right thing to do, that his experience with budgets and ideas would get the town away from looming bankruptcy. "You obviously know my dad."

"Bert has always been quite a character." She sighed and tipped her head to the side. "And your mom was a big supporter of our library. I'm really sorry for your loss."

He gave a short nod, still feeling the hole in his life where his mom should have been. He'd always thought he'd have time to reconcile with her. To make up for his youthful indiscretions. That's why he'd moved back to town after his mother died. Why it was important to win the election, to prove to his dad that he'd changed. Maybe he'd get the chance to do so that he'd lost with his mother.

He cleared his throat. "I'm sure she'd get a kick out of seeing me run for mayor." He glanced behind his shoulder at the city clerk, who watched them with a gleam of interest in her eyes. "By the way, Sandra seems to be convinced that I'm going to lose this election. You don't happen to know who I'm running against, do you?"

Shelby smiled wickedly. He was instantly suspicious and smiled. "Why, yes, I do. You're running against me."

SHELBY ENJOYED SEEING how Josh's jaw dropped at her news. Maybe he'd realize that he should pull out of the race now. Maybe he'd back out with grace rather than lose embarrassingly to her. She already had the support of Thora's small business association, half of the current town council and the PTA. She was the one who had stayed in Thora, while he'd run away not long after high school. She knew what Thora needed to succeed, not him. It was her duty to run for mayor. She'd been encouraged to do so by her family since she'd been a young girl. They expected her to not only run, but to win because that's what Cuthberts did.

And despite the man standing in front of her, she would be the next mayor.

He held out his hand. "May the best candidate win."

Then again, maybe he wouldn't concede.

She shook his hand and looked him in the eye. "Don't worry. I will."

He smiled and winked at her before leaving city hall. Shelby watched him go, thinking how much he had changed from his lanky teen days. His body had filled out nicely, but his cocky grin hadn't changed one bit.

"Can you believe that? Josh Riley running for mayor," Sandra said from her counter. "I'd never have believed it if I hadn't seen it with my own eyes."

Shelby went to the clerk's window and leaned on it. "Stranger things have happened in Thora. This just means that I need to step up my game."

"I wouldn't worry about Josh. Everyone remembers what he was like. Irresponsible, untrustworthy…"

Shelby did remember how he'd used her in high school, but she wasn't the same person that she'd been back then. Maybe

Josh wasn't either. "People can change their minds."

"But not their memories."

SHELBY RECOUNTED WHAT had happened to Melanie and Jack later that evening over dinner at their favorite Italian restaurant. Melanie twirled spaghetti carbonara onto her fork. "Josh Riley? After all these years?" She looked up from her plate and leaned in closer to Shelby. In a low whisper, she asked, "So how did he look?"

Too good. "Remember that superhero movie you took me to last month? And how we drooled over the villain who was dark but really dishy? Yeah, like that."

Melanie's eyebrows shot up and her lips made an 'oh' shape. "Yummy." She put a fork full of pasta into her mouth.

Jack wrinkled his nose at the topic of conversation. "So how will this change your campaign strategy?" When she and Melanie turned to look at him, he shrugged. "You've obviously thought about how you're going to beat him. You'll have to change tactics. Everybody loves a bad-boy-becomes-good-and-comes-back-home story."

Melanie nodded. "He's right. We can't assume that you're going to automatically win because Josh once had a reputation in this town. He returned to take care of his dad. That alone shows he's changed a little bit, at least. And the sympathy from that could earn him votes."

"Changed or not, he doesn't have the first clue about what it will take to help Thora. He's been gone too long." Shelby tapped her finger on the table. "I've been here my whole life. I know how things work and what we need to do to fix them."

"Which we will be sure to emphasize while out on the campaign trail." Melanie shifted her attention back to her dinner. "Besides organizing the door-to-door canvassing, I'm thinking we need to start preparing for the debate next month. We can have practice sessions at the store after hours." She swallowed another forkful of pasta and readied the next. "Jack, you'll help, of course."

His expression suddenly brightened. "I could pretend to be Josh."

Melanie eyed him up close. "From the

sounds of it, he's got you beat in the looks department."

"But not the smarts or the compassion or the—"

"We'll have to see about that, won't we?" Melanie said.

Shelby covered her smile with her napkin. She'd been watching her best friend, Melanie, and her cousin Jack flirt for ages, but they'd never dated. Not for lack of trying on Melanie's part. "I'd appreciate the practice. Thanks, Jack."

"Good. We'll start on Tuesday nights after the store has closed." Melanie pulled a small notebook and pen from her purse. "We'll have to come up with a better slogan for your yard signs and pamphlets."

"What's wrong with 'Shelby Knows Best'?" They had liked it when she'd come up with it a few months ago. With Josh entering the race, had her good ideas become dull? "We agreed that it would work."

"When you were running unopposed, yes. Now it makes you sound too cocky." Melanie wrote several things into the notebook and handed it to her. "We need to position you as the candidate who has the knowledge and the experience to lead Thora. We also need to emphasize the Cuthbert name. Your family has played a positive role in the town since it started."

Shelby read over Melanie's ideas. "This is why I'm glad you're my campaign manager. These are better than I came up with."

Melanie patted her hand. "This challenge isn't one we anticipated, but you don't have anything to worry about. Everyone expects you to win."

Jack gave a shrug. "What if Josh is a bigger problem than you're thinking?"

When Shelby and Melanie both stared at him, he held up his hands. "All I'm saying is that this isn't going to be the cakewalk you expected it to be. Sure, Josh has a reputation and he's been gone from Thora for a dozen years, but that doesn't mean he's not a threat. You need to get intel on where he's been since high school. What has he done? What's his job? What's behind his decision to run for mayor of a town he hasn't lived in for more than a decade?"

Shelby agreed and flipped to a blank page in the notebook to add all this. "I never would have thought of that stuff."

Shelby had a feeling that a few sleepless nights lay ahead of her.

JOSH CARRIED HIS empty dinner plate to the sink, scraped the last bits of peas and carrots into a plastic container, then rinsed the plate before placing it in the open dishwasher. He turned back to look at his dad, who poked his fork at a pea. "Come on, Dad. It's not going to hurt you to eat a green vegetable."

"You cooked it, so it might." His dad pushed his plate away. "I don't like peas."

"You didn't eat the carrots either." Josh finished packing up the leftovers from dinner. "If you're not going to eat it, bring your dinner plate to the sink."

"You don't need to boss me around." But his dad stood and carried over his dish and glanced at the plastic containers. "Keeping more of those vegetables to torture me with tomorrow?"

"I've been cooking for you since the beginning of the year, Dad. Have I poisoned you once?"

"Don't mean you won't try when you get a chance." He shuffled out to the living room, and Josh heard the television click to life.

After putting the food away, Josh started the dishwasher. Wiped down the table and kitchen counters, much as he had when he'd been a kid. Glancing around the dated room, he realized that nothing had changed since he'd left at eighteen. It made him wonder if he could change people's opinions of him.

Once the kitchen was clean, he joined his dad in the living room. His father sat in a recliner in front of the television. At least that piece of furniture was different. He'd probably worn out the rust-colored chair that had once been there. This new recliner didn't squeak when his dad pushed the bar on the side to raise the footrest, but it still had the afghan his mother had crocheted, which was older than Josh himself.

Josh took a seat on the couch and pulled out his cell phone, scrolling through emails while the news played on the television. He'd been doing pretty much the same thing every night since he'd moved back in just after the New Year. Over five months of sitting on the couch and thinking that he needed to make a change and not being sure of how to go about it. His dad wasn't getting better, and his heart certainly wasn't thawing toward Josh.

"You get those signatures you needed?"

Josh looked up at him. "Yes, I did. Surprised?"

The old man made a noise at the back of his throat. "What makes you think you can be mayor?"

"Night after night, I've listened to you complain about how the old mayor doesn't do anything. How his affair with the city attorney besmirched the dignity of the mayoral office. And how it's about time that somebody makes a difference in Thora." Josh tapped his chest. "Why not me?"

"Word around town is that Shelby Cuthbert is running too."

"You rarely leave the house. How are you getting news like that?"

His dad shrugged. "I've got my sources." He peered at Josh. "You really think you can run against Shelby and win?"

Those were his exact thoughts too. Shelby Cuthbert was practically Thora royalty. She'd been high school valedictorian. President of student council. As a freshman in high school, she'd started a petition to add more computers to the school's library, then raised enough funds to buy them. She had been a powerhouse back then. Twelve more years of experience might have made her even more unbeatable. He was in over his head. "I'm going to try."

His dad cackled and turned back to his program. Josh gritted his teeth. "Why is it so funny that I could win?"

"Besides the fact that you're always going to be a delinquent? Not much I can think of."

"I am not a delinquent." He rose to his feet and purposely stood in front of the television. When his dad protested, Josh pointed his finger. "I'm going to be the next mayor of Thora because I'm willing to do whatever it takes to win. Just you wait."

CHAPTER TWO

JOSH FLIPPED THE pages of the dated magazine and glanced up at the clock hanging on the wall above the receptionist's desk. The nurse had taken his dad back to get his blood drawn more than fifteen minutes ago, but the old man hadn't yet returned. Hoping that everything was okay, he threw the magazine back on to the worn wooden coffee table and retrieved his phone from his pants pocket to check his email.

The front door of the doctor's office opened, and Josh watched Shelby breeze in and approach the receptionist's desk. He slid down a little in the chair and picked up a magazine to cover his face, hoping she hadn't spotted him.

The frosted glass window slid open, and Lynda, the receptionist, smiled at Shelby. "I don't have you down for an appointment this morning, Shelby. Did I miss something?"

"No appointment, but I was hoping to drop off some campaign signs to post in front of your office building." She held up a handful of brochures. "I've also got some of my campaign literature to leave on the coffee table in the waiting room."

Josh peeked around the magazine to watch Shelby. He should have thought about bringing some campaign materials himself.

Lynda took the brochures. "Of course. I'll make sure Dr. Madorski approves them first, but I don't see why not."

"Thanks, Lynda."

She turned, and Josh found himself looking into her blue eyes. He gave her a nod. "Hi, Shelby."

She pulled the strap of her purse higher on to her shoulder and repeated his gesture. "Josh."

The door from the back opened, and Josh's dad appeared, a bandage securing a piece of gauze to his inner arm. "Why, Shelby, it's good to see you."

"You too, Mr. Riley. How do you like Josh being back in town?"

Josh peered at his dad, who smiled warmly at Shelby. "It's been interesting. He's always after me to eat my vegetables."

"You should listen to your son. Those vegetables are good for you."

His dad waved off the suggestion. "But what about you running for mayor of Thora? Isn't that something? Your granddad would be busting his buttons over you following in his footsteps."

Shelby noticed Josh's expression before returning her gaze back to his dad. "And I'm running against your son of all people."

"I wouldn't worry about that. Everyone in town knows that you're sure to win."

"Still, I'm positive that Josh will give me a challenge in the election."

His dad chuckled. "Well, my vote's on you, Shelby."

"Thank you, Mr. Riley." She smiled and patted his arm before nodding at Josh and leaving the office.

Josh helped his dad to sit down on the chair beside his. "Really, Dad?"

"What? Shelby is the perfect choice for mayor. She knows what she's talking about, been in this town her whole life, through its ups and downs. Besides, her family has been steering her toward the job practically since she was born."

"And you won't even consider voting for your own son?"

His dad gave him a sideways look. "If I knew that you were going to win against that girl, I might think about it. But everyone knows that she's going to win. What's the point of even trying?"

"Because I have good ideas for the town too. I know what it takes to mobilize a group of people to make positive changes in the community. And I have connections with industry people to bring big businesses to town." Josh shook his head and crossed his leg over one knee. "But then, you wouldn't know that about me, would you?"

"You do all that in Pittsburgh?"

Josh gave him a nod. "And more."

His dad looked him over. "You might want to let people know that about you."

"I'm trying, Dad. I'm trying."

AT THE WEEKEND Farmer's Market held in the front of the city hall, Shelby placed two large ripe tomatoes in the wicker basket hanging from her arm before turning to the huge heads of romaine, when she heard her mother approaching. "Hi, Mom."

Her mother gave a nod to the vendor behind the table. "I wasn't sure you'd heard me. I've been calling your name for the last few minutes."

"Have some things on my mind is all." She stepped around her mother, leaving the romaine and handing the farmer a few dollar bills for the tomatoes.

"Everyone's been talking about Josh Riley putting in his name for mayor."

Shelby scoffed. "That's hardly news anymore. It's been known for almost a week now."

"Do you know why he's running?"

Shelby bit her lip. "He hasn't said anything beyond having ideas on how to help Thora."

"What ideas? And how would he know what to do? You're the one who's been preparing for this your whole life."

Shelby could remember Pops whispering in her ear about growing up to be mayor one day. He had encouraged her to run for class president in fifth grade and had applauded when she'd been elected. He'd even taken her out for ice cream as a reward. *You're a chip off the old block*, her grandfather had told her over hot fudge sundaes. *Public service runs in your blood. You'll be mayor one day. Just you wait.*

And serving the public did run in the family. Pops had served as mayor at one time. One of her uncles had been police chief, and another was fire chief. Cuthberts had been expected to be bastions of the community, and she wasn't going to let their legacy end with them.

"Josh has the right to run for mayor as much as I do."

"Well, he doesn't have a chance of winning."

Shelby let her fingers linger on the cucumbers before turning back to her mother. "And I'll make sure of that."

Her mother smiled and reached over to rub her arm. "That's my girl."

They walked together for a moment, picking their produce, when her mother leaned over and hissed, "He's coming this way."

"Who?" Shelby looked up and found Josh walking toward them.

He smiled at them. "Mrs. Cuthbert. Shelby. I'd forgotten how busy the Farmer's Market tends to be first thing on Saturday morning, but I wanted to make sure to get the good stuff before it's gone."

"No one has better produce in June than here." She glanced at the tote bags in his hands. "More green vegetables to torture your dad with?"

Josh chuckled. "You'd think I was using broccoli to poison him or something."

Shelby's mom glanced between the two of them. "What's going on here?"

Shelby gave a shrug. "We're making small talk."

"You two have an inside joke already? I didn't know you knew each other that well."

Josh gave a shrug. "We saw each other at the doctor's office the other day."

"His dad doesn't like vegetables."

Her mother narrowed her eyes. "But you're running against each other for mayor."

As if Shelby didn't know that. "We can still be friendly."

Her mom looked Josh over, then pointed at him. "Shelby's going to win, you know? Everyone expects her to."

"Yes, ma'am."

"Mom." Shelby shook her head. "This isn't the time for that."

Her mom looked like she was about to say something else, but then pursed her lips together. "Shelby, we'll see you tomorrow for dinner after church?"

Shelby nodded and gave her mother a kiss on the cheek. "Why don't I bring a veggie tray with what I'm buying here?"

"One o'clock then." She pointed once more at Josh. "She's going to win."

After her mom left, Shelby glanced at Josh and shrugged. "Sorry about that. She's my biggest supporter."

"And not the only one. No less than five people made a point to tell me that you'll be the next mayor between getting out of the car and entering the market."

"Thora's citizens tend to have strong opinions."

"But are more than willing to let others do the work for them."

Shelby started to say something, but changed her mind. It wasn't the time for this type of a debate. "I think people are wait-ing for a leader to show them what can be achieved. You might be surprised what will happen with the right person in charge."

"Leader...meaning you."

She inclined her head. "If the voters choose me, then yes. I know that I can make a difference in Thora."

Josh gave a soft smile that made her insides quiver. "From what I hear, I think you already have. Is there a committee that you haven't volunteered for?"

She returned his smile and found herself staring into his eyes for a second too long. What was she doing? This was Josh Riley. She cleared her throat as if to tidy her thoughts, as well. "I should get going." She glanced into his tote bag, then pointed to one of the vendors. "They have fresh green beans on special over there. I'm sure your dad would appreciate those."

Josh laughed and briefly touched her elbow before following her advice. She watched him go, wondering about him. And what she was going to do with this annoying attraction that seemed to have flared up between them.

SHELBY PLACED HER hands first on the makeshift podium that Mel had created out of a stack of books. Then she reached over to adjust her three-by-five note cards. "Don't fidget," Melanie said as she set up another pile for Jack. "It makes you look nervous, and voters want a candidate who exudes confidence."

"But I am nervous."

"Fine. Just don't show it. This is our third practice session. This shouldn't be a big deal by now."

Shelby folded her hands. "The debate is in ten days. Do you think I'll be ready by then?"

"Let's be honest. You're ready now. These practice sessions are just meant to get you to shed your nerves."

"You sound like a self-help book."

Melanie pointed to another stack that she'd placed behind the counter. "Where do you think I got the advice?"

Shelby flipped through the volumes, reading the titles. "And we're going to find the answers we need in here?"

"I not only sell books. I read them too. So yes. I believe all the answers we need are in there somewhere." Melanie gestured at the clock behind the cash register. "Where's Jack? We did say seven thirty, right?"

"Maybe he had a last-minute emergency at the clinic." Her cousin had been known to miss plans due to a veterinary crisis or two. It wasn't unusual for her and Melanie to go on without him.

"If that was the case, he would call or text."

True, he may not show up, but at least he'd let them know. Shelby looked at her friend. "Speaking of Jack, any change on that front?"

"We're not talking about me and Jack tonight. This is all about getting you to kick some behind at the debate. I've been going over my notes from the last practice. You should start depending less on the cards and more on your presence."

Shelby picked up her note cards and read through them again. She'd laid out her plan for increasing tax revenues by attracting small business owners to Thora with tax incentives. Businesses and families were a key part of her plan. She placed the cards back on the podium and sighed. Mel was right. She knew the plan forward and backward by now, but having the cards felt like a safety net. "Josh was a great debater in high school. He might not have been prepared for class, but he could talk anyone into anything. I doubt that has changed."

"So we will win the crowd over with facts." Melanie grasped Shelby by her upper arms. "Where is my strong, confident best friend? You've got this."

Shelby nodded, trying to convince herself. With Josh entering the mayoral race as an unknown quantity, she was suddenly doubting her strengths. Could she win this race?

Yes, she could. Because she had to. The future of Thora was in jeopardy.

"You're right. I know what I'm going to say. I need a formidable stage presence. Maybe one that will intimidate Josh."

"Instead of the other way around? Exactly."

"He doesn't intimidate me." When Mel scoffed at her statement, Shelby muttered to herself, "Maybe just a little."

A knock on the locked front door of the bookstore alerted them to Jack's arrival. He breezed in when Melanie opened up. Waving a large envelope, he said, "Sorry

I'm late, but I was waiting on this information. Remember I asked the other night where Josh has been these last years? Well, now we know." He opened the envelope and placed several sheets of paper on the counter. "Pittsburgh."

Shelby picked up one of the pages and read it over, her eyebrows rising at the short profile from a well-known computer magazine. "He owns an app-design firm?"

"Owned. Past tense. He recently sold it for big money before he moved back here." He handed her a different article that detailed the sale of Josh's business. "It explains why he can stay here indefinitely and not work a regular nine-to-five while he cares for Bert."

Shelby read the article and handed it to Melanie. "I remember that he was into computers, but I never pictured him as a big businessman or a nerd-type, creating apps."

"Maybe you don't know him as well as you think you did."

Obviously. Shelby perused the rest of the information. "And he won Pittsburgh's Citizen of the Year a couple years ago?" She shook her head. She really didn't know this Josh. "He sponsored STEM programs in schools and headed a commission with Pittsburgh's mayor to help address youth issues." She sighed and slapped the envelope onto the counter. "His mom never mentioned any of this."

"Maybe she didn't know." Melanie looked at her. "You remember how critical his parents were. Maybe he didn't tell them."

"This explains where he's been, but we still don't understand why he's running for mayor." Jack collected the information and put it back into the envelope. "I'll keep digging."

Melanie gave him a thumbs-up. "And in the meantime, let's practice for the debate. We need you to be clear and concise about why you're the best candidate for mayor. When the time comes, focus on one or two people in the audience so it doesn't overwhelm you. For now, concentrate on me, okay?" When Shelby didn't answer, her friend nudged her. "Don't let this information intimidate you. He's still been gone for a long time. He doesn't know the town as well as you."

Shelby took a deep breath and picked up

her note cards, then cocked her head to the side. "Who would have guessed that Thora's favorite bad boy would become Pittsburgh's citizen of the year? How much else have I missed?"

Melanie snapped her fingers in front of Shelby's face. "Focus. First question. What about your experiences make you prepared to be the new mayor of Thora?"

JOSH LOOKED ACROSS the picnic table at the cop. His old friend, Tim Kehoe, who had become a police officer after graduation, looked back at him. "What do you say? Will you be my campaign manager? Make it official?"

Tim ran a finger around the rim of his beer bottle. "Why are you asking me now and not when I convinced you to run?"

"Because I didn't think I'd need a campaign manager. But with running against Shelby Cuthbert, I've discovered that I need all the help I can get. And you're the perfect choice. You know Thora a lot better than I do. You've seen what the current mayor has done to it and the police force. You're also a homeowner who has kids in Thora's schools. All that gives you a vested interest in the future of our town."

Tim rested his arm on the table and looked out into the backyard where his children played, running through a sprinkler. "I never figured you would come back after your fancy life in Philadelphia."

"Pittsburgh."

"Whatever. Charmaine told me that you sold your company for big bucks."

Company? He had been working in a dank, smelly basement for ages until his golf app had gone viral five years ago. He'd finally moved into an office building and hired a receptionist so he could focus on the next big app. But when his mom died, he knew he had to return to Thora, and that meant selling the business to an investor who had eyed it for many months. "Something like that. You're the one who convinced me to run for mayor in the first place, so will you do this or not?"

"Sure. Like you said, I'll be your Thora connection. I know what we need and how to get it done." Tim sipped his beer. "We'll have to make a splash on the Fourth of July when things really kick off. I'm talking the parade. Shaking a bunch of hands. And then the debate before the fireworks." Tim peered at him. "When's the last time you were in a debate?"

"Junior year of high school. So I'm going to need lots of practice." He paused as he thought about his opponent. "Do I have a chance against Shelby Cuthbert?"

"The Cuthberts think they run everything in this town, but I'll let you in on a little secret." Tim leaned closer. "Their time is over. New folks like you and me are exactly what's needed to make a difference."

"That's what I'm hoping to do. Make a difference." Josh pulled his beer bottle forward. "But you didn't answer my question about Shelby. Do I have a chance?"

"Honestly?" Tim winced. "You've got a long way to go and a rough road ahead."

That's what he was afraid of. "Then why am I running?"

"Everybody loves Shelby, but you and I are going to change all that."

He glanced up at Charmaine, who placed a bowl of chips on the table between them before carrying an armful of towels toward the kids. "I want to win this fair and square. I won't play dirty."

"You won't need to. She's nice and all, I guess, but she's not mayor material. She's planning on running on her family name, but it's not as pristine as it used to be."

"I'm trusting you, Tim."

"You don't have anything to worry about, future Mr. Mayor." Tim saluted him with his beer bottle.

THE DOOR SLAMMED in Josh's face before he could get out his entire spiel. "Thank you for your time," he yelled and then stepped off the porch. He made a quick mark on his clipboard. He'd visited almost two dozen houses and had gotten welcomed into only one. Still, he had a lot more on his list to call on.

The next house had a well-manicured lawn with lush green grass. Obviously, someone had spent a lot of time in the yard to make it look so nice. He walked up the sidewalk and took a deep breath before opening the screen door and knocking.

An elderly man opened the door and stared at him. "Can I help you, young man?"

Josh swallowed hard. "Mr. Hooks, right? You used to teach math at Thora High."

The man looked him over with squinted eyes, then broke into a smile. "Josh Riley, I'd heard that you were back in town." They shook hands before Mr. Hooks stepped back and waved Josh inside. "Come on in and out of the heat."

Josh thanked him as he stepped into the cool interior. The house looked much like the lawn had. Well kept and pristine. Not a thing out of place. "I didn't realize this is where you lived."

"My daughter's house, but she had me move in with her family after my heart attack a few years ago."

Josh frowned. "Are you okay?"

"Sure, sure. But that's not why you knocked on the front door." Mr. Hooks took a seat in an overstuffed armchair and motioned for Josh to take the other. "What brings you by?"

"I'm running for mayor and going door-to-door to drum up support." Josh pulled out one of the brochures he'd had printed that explained his platform to bring in big businesses to improve the economy in

Thora and handed it to Mr. Hooks. "I hope you'll consider voting for me."

Mr. Hooks read the pamphlet and nodded. "You've come a long way from high school." He looked up at Josh. "How did Pitt treat you?"

"Better than I deserved." Josh sat forward on the chair. "I never did thank you for all you did for me back then. If you hadn't put in a good word to the admissions officer for me, I don't know what would have happened."

"You would have found your way eventually. You're a smart kid. One of the brightest I ever had." Josh gave him a look, but the old man held firm. "I'm serious. You might have had a wild streak in you, but it wasn't because you weren't bright. Quite the opposite. It was because you were too bright. You needed a steady hand and some direction to channel that intelligence."

"Pitt certainly did that. It also gave me the fresh start that I needed." He'd been headed down a dark path when Mr. Hooks had him for precalculus and changed everything. He'd been able to see beyond Josh's exterior to something valuable underneath.

"No one would ever believe that I'd be back in Thora and running for mayor."

Mr. Hooks looked him over. "Why mayor? Of all the things you could do, why run for political office? You could have more of an impact in the private sector."

"That's a good question."

"One you'd better have an answer for if you're planning on winning, don't you think?"

"Maybe I should have hired you as my campaign manager." Josh sat back in the comfortable chair, considering his response. "I don't want to be bogged down in petty arguments and trivial squabbles. I want to make a real difference, and for me, that means being mayor. Finding the best policies. Setting a direction and taking the steps to get Thora where it needs to be. If I'm just bringing my own business to Thora, it's for my own benefit and not the town's."

Mr. Hooks smiled. "Good answer. You might want to write that down."

A knock on the front door caught their attention. Mr. Hooks took a moment to get up out of the deep chair and make it to the entrance. "Well, this is a pleasant surprise. What brings you here today?"

"I was hoping to talk to you about the mayoral race."

Josh winced. That sounded a lot like Shelby. Was she campaigning too? No wonder so many doors had been shut in his face. It was like Tim had said. Shelby was loved in this town. And if not loved, at least respected and admired. She was a go-getter. Strong and confident. She knew how to get things done.

"That is intriguing," Mr. Hooks told her. "Why don't you step inside so we can all talk about it?"

When Shelby entered the living room, Josh stood and gave her a nod. She narrowed her eyes at him. "What are you doing here?"

"Same thing as you. Trying to convince a voter that I'm the next mayor."

She turned to Mr. Hooks. "I didn't realize that you had company. I'll come back at another, more convenient time."

"There's no reason why we can't all discuss this." Mr. Hooks motioned to the sofa.

"Why don't you take a seat while I get us something to drink? Iced tea?"

Shelby thanked him as Josh nodded. "Sounds great."

Shelby took a seat on the sofa and the furthest one from him. When Mr. Hooks left the living room to get their drinks, she faced Josh. "What's your angle? Are you looking for an endorsement from the chairman of the Garden Club?"

"The what? I just figured it's been a while since people have seen me, so I'm going door to door and talking to people. They need to know who I am now and what I stand for."

"And how's that going for you?"

She seemed genuinely interested, but Josh wasn't sure he was buying this naive act of hers. He took a while to answer her. "Not that great, to be honest."

Her gaze on him didn't waver, and he felt as if she was trying to figure him out. Finally, she said, "And you're still sure about running against me?"

"You're not the only one who has good ideas for Thora, Shelby. I have just as much experience as you to bring to the table. I think you'd be surprised to discover that."

Mr. Hooks reentered the room, and Shelby stood and rushed to him, helping him place the tray of drinks on to the coffee table. "Thank you for your help. You always were ready to lend a hand in my class."

"Anytime, Mr. Hooks."

She waited until he had seated himself before handing him a glass of iced tea. She then handed one to Josh. He looked up at her as he took it, one finger touching her hand before she pulled back as if she'd been burned. They sipped in silence for a while until Mr. Hooks cleared his throat. "So, who is going to try to convince me first?"

Josh waved his hand at Shelby. "Ladies first."

She turned her body so that her full attention was on Mr. Hooks. Josh watched her profile as she laid out the reasons that Thora needed her in charge. She'd changed so much since high school. Then, she'd been an awkward teenager in braces and glasses who had the tendency to follow the rules and shun those like him who had flouted them instead. But now, her beauty was eclipsed by only her confidence. By the time she finished speaking, she had almost convinced him to vote for her.

He didn't know how long he sat staring at her, but suddenly he became aware that Mr. Hooks and Shelby had both shifted in his direction. *Say something*, his brain prompted. He uttered the first thing that came into his head. "You always thought you knew everything in high school, but you were wrong then and you're wrong now."

"Excuse me?"

"Maybe *wrong* isn't the right word. More like *nearsighted*."

"That's how you're planning to defeat me? Personal attacks?"

"I'm not attacking you. I'm merely stating the fact that your plan for revitalizing Thora lacks depth. You're going to need more than small businesses to increase tax revenues."

"And what would you know about Thora's economy?"

"Not as much as I should, I'll admit, but I've been learning more as I delve into this campaign. Your problem is a simple matter of math. Small businesses won't bring enough revenue to add to Thora's bottom line."

Shelby gaped at him for several moments, then stood and placed her glass of iced tea back on the tray. "Thank you, Mr. Hooks, for the tea, but I need to be going."

"Don't run away, Shelby," Josh called after her retreating figure. He gave his excuses to Mr. Hooks, then hurried after her, catching up with her at her car, parked at the curb. He held on to the frame so that she couldn't close her door and leave. "Let's discuss this."

She tried to pry his fingers off. "We can talk about this at the debate." He must have paled at her words, because she gave him a triumphant grin. "See you then."

He let go of her door, and she slammed it shut before starting the engine and driving away. When he returned to Mr. Hooks's home, he knocked again on the front door. Mr. Hooks opened it for him and ushered him back to the living room. "I didn't mean to rattle her like that."

Mr. Hooks gave a nod. "If you ask me, it was about time someone did."

"So you're not voting for her?"

"I didn't say that." Mr. Hooks sipped his tea, then smiled warmly at him. "Let's hear your ideas."

SHELBY SLAMMED HER purse on the counter by the register at Melanie's bookstore. Scraping a stool back to take a seat near the coffee bar, she said, "Give me the hard stuff."

Melanie raised one eyebrow but didn't ask her anything as she made a full-fat latte with extra whipped cream and set it before Shelby. "Do you want to talk about it?"

"Who does he think he is, attacking my ideas like that? He's the one who's been absent all these years. I'm the one who's been around, working to help the town. Raising money when it was needed. Volunteering when it was called for. Leading committees when no one else would." She took a wood stick and started to stir the milky froth into the coffee, frowning into its depths. "Called me nearsighted. And said that my plan lacks depth." She took a sip of her drink. "Ha. He's the one who lacks depth."

"I hope this isn't how you're going to react during the debate."

Shelby looked up at Melanie. "Do you think my plan lacks depth?"

"No." She took a lid off a glass jar and used tongs to take out an almond biscotti and placed it on a napkin before handing it to Shelby. "You've done the research, so you've got the facts that back up everything you're saying. He's trying to fluster you. And succeeding, from the sounds of it."

Shelby thanked her for the cookie and placed it on the counter next to her coffee. "Why did I let him get to me like that?"

"Good question. Why did you?" Melanie peered at her, and Shelby tried not to glance away. "Are you still harboring a crush on him?"

That was almost laughable. Over a decade had passed since she'd last laid eyes on him. Out of sight, out of mind.

But he hadn't been out of mind. And seeing him now had seemed to resurrect her teenaged hormonal response to him.

That's what it was. Hormones. She was not a gawky adolescent looking for approval and assuming that her wild emotions meant love. She had matured past that point long ago. Who she was now couldn't be swayed by pretty eyes and a wide smile.

She shook her head. "No, I'm not."

"Good."

"But I have learned a couple things we can use." She took a bite of her cookie, then borrowed a pen from Melanie to write on the napkin, chewing as she reflected on their exchange. "He assumes my plan is all about attracting small businesses to add to the bottom line, so I'm sure he'll be preparing his attacks in the debate in kind. He doesn't know about what else I have prepared." She took another nibble and wrote down another idea. "He also thinks that this is about tax revenues for the city."

"Which does play a big part."

"True, but it's not the only thing." Shelby scribbled a few more lines and looked up at her friend. "This is also about restoring integrity to the office of mayor. Reestablishing the trust that was lost after our current mayor's affair. This is about character as much as it is about making money for the town."

"I won't let you hurt your own reputation by slinging personal attacks against Josh."

"We don't have to hit him on that front. But we need to change some of my speeches about my own character. Play up my family's reputation and history with the town. Show how I won't let politics and money change who I am as a person."

Melanie used the tongs to bring out another cookie and sampled it. "By emphasizing your own integrity, the voters will question his, in other words. And you do it without a single word against him."

"Exactly."

"But what if he is just as honorable as you?"

That was the risk. She'd seen the articles that had lauded his efforts when he won Citizen of the Year. He was a champion for kids and education. A successful entrepreneur.

But could the boy who had left a trail of broken hearts and graffitied walls have transformed so much? Could a leopard not just change the spots that marred him, but remove them once and for all?

"My aunts and uncles are hosting a barbecue for interested voters at Uncle Bob's house tomorrow night. I'm going to shake hands. Give a short speech. Can you come?"

"Will Jack be there?"

"It's his parents' house, so yes. Unless some veterinary emergency pulls him away."

Mel bit into her own biscotti. "Happy to."

JOSH MOVED THE lawnmower to the shed in the backyard before returning to the garage, where Tim had set up a long table with folding chairs around it. "Remind me why we're doing this again."

Tim adjusted a seat. "To see you elected, we need to get your name out there. You're only one person with the same twenty-four hours in a day that we all have, so we bring in volunteers to talk about you to other potential voters." He counted the chairs and seemed frustrated with the result. "Shelby has her entire family campaigning for her, so who do you know that we can ask to work for you?"

He paused. Unlike Shelby, he didn't have an army of people who loved him that he could solicit. "I could see if some of my dad's friends would volunteer."

"What about your dad?"

Josh glanced over his shoulder to find the old man watching them from the kitchen window. "He's not exactly my biggest fan."

"What would it hurt to suggest it? He might surprise you and agree to help."

Josh debated the wisdom of asking his father, but the worst that could happen is the old man would say no. He let out a long breath before leaving Tim to finish working on the garage.

When he entered the house, Josh discovered that his dad had left the window and returned to his recliner and the television. "I was wondering if you'd be interested in working with me on my campaign."

His dad's head jerked back before shaking from side to side. "I'm too busy."

"With what? Watching your shows all day?"

"I got plans you don't know about."

"For example?"

"Plans with my buddy, Roy."

"When?"

"None of your business."

Josh raised one eyebrow and stared at his dad. "If you don't want to help me out, just say so."

His dad looked him in the eyes. "Fine. I don't want to."

"That's what I thought." Josh turned and left his old man alone.

He paused in the hallway, then turned to find his dad staring at the television. Since Josh had come home, his dad had spent the majority of his time in the recliner with that TV set to a program that Josh doubted he actually watched. It was noise and a distraction from the absence of his mom. Instead of filling that hole with his son, however, his dad had chosen to fill it with flickering images of people that he'd never know.

Josh closed his eyes for a moment, wishing that he could reach his dad. Isn't that why he'd returned home in the first place?

But instead of getting closer, they seemed to be drifting further apart.

Josh gathered what courage he had left and reentered the living room. "I have to get volunteers for my campaign."

"So why are you looking at me?"

"I was hoping you'd have some ideas of people that I can ask."

His dad seemed more surprised by that request than when he'd asked if he wanted to work on the campaign himself. "I'm busy right now."

"Please, Dad. Your cop show can wait." Josh took a seat on the sofa.

His dad lowered the volume on the television. "I could ask Roy if he knows anyone. And if he doesn't, I'm sure his wife, Trudy, does."

"Thanks, Dad. I'd appreciate that."

"You're really going through with this mayor thing, then?"

Josh nodded. "I think I could do some good things for the town."

"They're going to eat you alive, you know? The Cuthberts are huge here, and they don't like outsiders who go up against one of their own."

"I realize that, but I have to try." Josh stood and put a hand on his dad's shoulder. "Thanks for helping me out."

His dad grumbled as Josh left the room, smiling. It wasn't much of a start, but it was something at least.

SHELBY CIRCULATED AMONG the people her aunts and uncles had invited for the barbecue, an iced tea in her hand and a smile on her face. She leaned forward to hear better what Mr. Ledbetter was saying since the din of the crowd had risen as the night had gone on. She nodded as he finished speaking. "I agree with you that the new mayor needs to be honorable. That's where transparency comes in. And that's why I'm going to make sure my office is open to all citizens, at all times."

Mr. Ledbetter seemed pleased with her answer and stepped away to let the next person who was waiting to talk to her have access. Instead of seeing one of Uncle Bob's friends, however, she stared into Josh's eyes. "What are you doing here?"

He gave a shrug. "I was invited, along with my dad."

She narrowed her eyes. "By who?"

"Roy and Trudy Krauseneck. They're friends of my father's." He pointed to an older couple who were talking with Josh's dad and Uncle Mark near the back of the yard.

"And they didn't see the irony of bringing you to *my* campaign event?"

"When they mentioned that your uncle was grilling ribs, I was all in." He gazed around the crowd that filled the backyard. "This is a nice turn out. Good for you, Shelby."

"Yes, it is. Now you can go home?"

"But I haven't had my ribs yet." He gave her a wink and moved on toward Mrs. Ledbetter who was waving him over.

Shelby took a deep breath. She wasn't going to let Josh's presence get to her. In fact, she'd turn it to her advantage. But how?

Aunt Jeri put a hand on her shoulder and gave her an affectionate squeeze. "I did not invite that man here tonight."

"I know, Auntie. It's fine."

"But Bob is going to ask him to speak to the group too. You know how your uncle is about playing fair."

Shelby let out a rush of air. She couldn't let Josh fluster her like this in front of potential voters. She needed to present a poised, calm demeanor that exuded confidence and leadership.

But maybe this was exactly what she'd been hoping for. "That just means I have to be more articulate and charming than he is. Out talk him, so to speak." She shared a smile with her aunt. "Luckily, I bet I can do just that."

CHAPTER THREE

THE SMELL OF bacon wafted through the large tent. Shelby grinned, please to see the griddles manned by Christopher Fox, Shelby's cousin's fiancé. He wore a large red apron that read Vote for Shelby and matched those worn by other members of her extended family. Her parents, cousins, aunts and uncles circulated among the folks seated at the folding tables near the park gazebo.

Her great-aunt Sarah made sure that all the bottles of syrup stayed filled while her aunt June poured cups of orange juice. Even her cousin Kristine had made an appearance before she had to go in to work at the beauty salon.

Based on the number of full tables, her fundraising pancake breakfast was a success. The donated funds would help her family's charity, which provided Christmas gifts for children who might not otherwise get them. It had been a considerable expense to set up the pancake breakfast, but her campaign coffers could afford it. And it went a long way to prove her commitment to the town.

Someone called her name, and she walked over in that direction, a smile on her face. "I hope you're enjoying these amazing pancakes."

Mrs. McClelland, her old French teacher, pointed to her husband's empty plate and chair. "He's going back for thirds." She motioned toward the crowd. "You should be proud of everything you're doing."

"I am."

"And you shouldn't be upset that your opponent is holding his own pancake breakfast on the other side of the park."

Shelby felt her smile droop. "Josh is doing what?"

"My husband said that your pancakes are better than his, so I wouldn't worry."

Shelby thanked her and strode directly to Melanie, who was refilling bottles with maple syrup. Her friend sighed. "Uh-oh. What did he do now?"

"How do you know I'm upset about Josh?"

"You get that little wrinkle in the space between your eyebrows when it comes to him."

Shelby tried to fix her expression. "Did you know he's having a pancake breakfast too? We reserved this park months ago for the fundraiser. How was he able to get a permit so quickly?"

Melanie put her hands on Shelby's upper arms. "First of all, take a deep breath."

She closed her eyes and shook her head.

"May I remind you that your voters are watching your reaction right now?"

Shelby turned to find more than two dozen pairs of eyes on her. She took a deep breath, smiled and gave a small wave. When she faced Melanie, she dropped the smile as well as the volume of her voice. "I'm going over there. He has no business not only copying my idea but holding his event at the same time as mine!"

"Shh. Listen, as your campaign manager, I strongly recommend that you stay put. Visit with the crowd that's here. I'm going to check on the bacon. I see Jack is distracting Christopher with some crazy, funny story."

Shelby knew she was right. Josh having his own fundraising breakfast wasn't unusual for the start of the town's Fourth of July celebration weekend. But to have it at the same park, at the same time? It was like he was thumbing his nose at her.

Before she changed her mind, Shelby stalked across the grounds to find Josh wearing an apron and chef's hat, posing for the newspaper's photographer. She stood watching, arms over her chest. Part of her was thrilled to see that his tables weren't as full as hers.

When the photographer finished, Josh turned to Shelby, smiling. "Hungry?"

"Don't start with me."

"Uh-oh. You're upset." He walked toward her, taking the chef's hat off his head. "What is it now?"

"Who approved your permit for this?"

Josh's eyes widened. "I needed a permit?" When she started to bristle, he laughed. "I'm kidding, Shelby. My campaign manager got it a week ago at city hall. This is all on the up and up. I promise."

"But I filed my permit months ago. The town's bylaws allow only one permit at a time to avoid overcrowding and damage to the park. They had to institute that rule after the competing music festival fiasco three years ago." She shook her head at the memory. Cars had crowded the surrounding streets so homeowners hadn't been able to leave or return because of it. And it had taken weeks to clean up the area, a project she'd spearheaded. "But then, you wouldn't know that, since you've been gone."

"Obviously, the clerk's office thought that two pancake breakfasts wouldn't ruin the park."

He didn't understand the gravity of this situation. Her fingers twitched, and it felt as if the ends of her hair were standing straight up from her head. This anger that he provoked surged inside her until…until… "This is just like how you hijacked my uncle's barbecue."

"I was invited to the barbecue just like everyone else."

"But it was held in *my* honor by *my* family."

He gave a shrug. "It's not my fault that your uncle was kind enough to ask me to speak too. You should be glad to have the competition. They seemed to like what you had to say."

"You think this is funny?"

"A little bit." He smirked at her. "You're really cute when you're angry. Has anyone ever told you that?"

The words made her mouth drop open as she stared at him. "Are you trying to be condescending or does it just come naturally to you?"

"Wow. You're sure ready for our debate, with a quick comeback like that."

"Well, if you'd grown up since I last saw you, quick comebacks wouldn't be necessary."

He stepped closer to her, the smile in his eyes dimming. "Don't assume that I haven't grown up. You don't know me. Not anymore."

"You don't know me either."

Someone cleared their throat behind Shelby. She turned to find Christopher standing there. "I hate to break up this private conversation, but we have a problem."

JOSH FOLLOWED SHELBY back to the other side of the park despite her protests that she didn't need his help. He hadn't meant to be condescending, but she glowed when she was angry, and it made him like her all the more. He couldn't help it.

He shouldn't be thinking like that, not when she was his political rival. He also shouldn't notice her figure or the way the apron looked flattering on her. *Get your head in the game, Riley. She might be more attractive when she's upset, but you're the one she's angry at.*

Melanie Beach stood near the large tent, her hand sheltering her eyes as they approached. She gave him a look but then addressed Shelby. "Jack's looking at the breakers to see if we blew a fuse, but he doesn't see an issue."

Josh held up a finger. "I might be able to help with that."

Shelby glared at him. "You're an electrician as well as a citizen of the year?"

She knew about his award? He'd have to think about that later. "Actually, I worked on a construction crew for a while on my summer breaks, and we blew enough fuses for me to learn how to fix them. Where's the generator?"

Shelby pointed to where her cousin Jack stood peering into the equipment. When Josh walked up behind him, Jack turned and lowered his cell phone, which he'd been using as a flashlight. "What are you doing here?"

"Could I take a look?"

Jack moved aside. Josh squatted down beside the unit and twisted off the screws to the cover of the voltage regulator. He followed the wires and saw that one of the leads had come loose. Tightening it, he hoped that would resolve the issue.

The generator sputtered to life and the crowd cheered. Josh replaced the cover and screws, then dusted off his hands as he stood. "Sounds like you're all set."

Shelby moved past him to stare down at the unit. "Just like that?"

She turned to look at him, and he realized her face was inches away from his. The freckles that had once spotted her cheeks had faded into a peaches-and-cream complexion. He swallowed at the rush of attraction that once again flared. "Y-yes. Just like that. Sometimes it's the small answers that solve the bigger problems."

"Well, thanks." The corners of her mouth twitched, and then she whirled away and rejoined her family.

The man who had retrieved Shelby earlier held out his hand. "Thank you, Josh."

Josh shook it. "You don't look like a Cuthbert. How are you associated with Shelby?"

"I'm Christopher Fox, but I'm engaged to a Cuthbert." He pointed to a woman with wavy blond hair, watching them from the tent. "That's Penny with my kids."

"She's the firefighter. I've heard about her."

Christopher smiled like a man in love. "That would be her." He waved to his fiancée, then focused again on Josh. "I've heard about you too. And not just about running for mayor against Shelby."

"Oh?" That didn't sound promising.

"You have quite the reputation."

"Had. Whatever you heard was from more than a decade ago." Was no one going to give him a chance to show that he wasn't the same boy that he'd been then? "I've changed."

"You came to Shelby's rescue without

hesitating. That says a lot to me." Christopher gave him a nod, returning to the tent.

When Josh reached his side of the park, he saw Tim raise his hands in a gesture asking where he'd disappeared to. Josh shook his head as if it wasn't any big deal.

Which it hadn't been. He'd simply offered a quick solution for someone with a problem. But it had felt like more than that.

It had felt like a small step toward redemption.

THE EARLY MORNING heat of the Fourth of July blazed the back of Shelby's neck.

"I think you got the imaginary spot," Melanie said from behind her.

Shelby straightened but still ran the chamois along the hood of her 1967 Mustang for a final swipe. "I want it to be perfect for the parade."

"It already is."

Melanie handed Shelby a bottle of water that might have once been cold, but the heat and humidity had started to turn it warm. It dripped with condensation. Shelby twisted the cap off and took a long guzzle. She needed to keep hydrated if she was going to last the day. The parade began at ten, followed by her family's cookout, then the debate at the gazebo that evening and the annual fireworks to end the holiday.

She threw the chamois into the back seat of the car and opened the driver's-side door. "Did you see what Josh is driving in the parade?"

"I've been too focused on you and your campaign to care."

Shelby knew that was the right attitude. She shouldn't be so concerned about what Josh was or wasn't doing. Even after he'd come to her rescue the day before, she still didn't trust him. Their history made her wary.

And who could blame her? She'd waited on her front porch in a frilly dress for three hours on prom night before realizing that he wasn't showing. That his asking her had been a joke.

Some joke.

Though he didn't leave town until after graduation, she never confronted him about it. She kept changing her mind. One minute, she was too afraid of what the answer might be, the next minute, she convinced herself she didn't care what the answer was.

Although, thinking of the Josh he seemed to be now, the one who'd come to her aid, made her question her old attitude. In the past, he would have laughed and said some kind of snide comment about her messed-up breakfast and left her to it. *Had he really changed?*

She looked around the busy parking lot of the high school, the staging area where the parade would begin. The gardening club fussed over its float covered with brightly colored plants and flowers and a flag on each corner. The high school marching band warmed up in unison. The dance academy had kids dressed in sparkly costumes and performing cartwheels and gymnastics. The city council members had donned historical costumes and carried red, white and blue buckets full of candy to throw to the spectators.

"Hey, Shel." Her cousin Penny put an arm around one of her shoulders. "Do you know what order we're supposed to line up in for this thing?"

She pointed to a tall man with a clipboard

that barked orders to a group of clowns. "You have to check in with the recreation director, Lou."

"I figured you'd be the one in charge."

"Not this year. Since I'm in the parade, I had to hand over the reins to someone else."

"Got it." Penny gave a wave and headed toward Lou.

Shelby glanced at her watch. It was ten minutes until the parade was to kick off, but chaos reigned instead. No one had lined up. Members of the quilting bee were still trying to straighten their quilt of the Liberty Bell. They'd worked on it for three months straight. And then, there was the men's chorus, unorganized and only just warming up their voices. The first few strains of "The Stars and Stripes Forever" filled the warm air. Now, if she was in charge…

Melanie groaned. "I know that look, but you need to trust Lou with this. You can't control the world."

"We should at least have the first three groups lined up in order by now."

"Let it go."

"You know how hard that is for me."

Melanie made a noise in the back of her

throat but didn't comment further. Instead, she checked the magnetic signs on the side of the Mustang that invited citizens to vote for Shelby. Her campaign also had placed signs along the parade route. No one in Thora would be able to claim they didn't know she was running for mayor.

"Are you planning on coming to the family cookout at Christopher's after?"

Before Melanie could answer, Josh sauntered over and placed a hand along the Mustang, whistling. "This is some car. Is it the same one you were restoring in high school?"

He remembered that? "You don't get rid of a classic like this."

His smile lit up his entire face, and Shelby forgot what she had been about to say. He had smiled at her like that years ago, but now his face sported a few wrinkles around the corners of his eyes. It made him even more good-looking.

Wanting to smack her head for having such thoughts about her political rival, Shelby instead frowned at the parking lot, searching for his car. "What are you driving in the parade?"

"Tim said that walking would make me more visible. Plus, this way, I can shake more hands along the route. More one-to-one interaction."

Why hadn't she thought of that? But then, Josh needed to get more face time with people. Shelby knew most of Thora's citizens, having spent her whole life in this town. Her name was one they recognized. One they trusted.

And that would help her win.

"Well, it looks like we're finally starting to line up." She opened the driver's door and paused. "Good luck in the debate tonight."

"Same to you."

She watched Josh walk away, then turned to find Melanie studying her. "Is something wrong? What did I say?"

"You like him."

"You're joking, right?" She got into the car and waited as her friend walked around the Mustang and got into the passenger side. "This is Josh you're talking about."

"Exactly. You had a major crush on that bad boy all through high school."

"Ancient history."

"Is it? Because the look on your face

when you were talking to him just now seems to say otherwise. I thought your frustration with him was because he was running against you, but I'm not so sure."

"What else would it be?"

"Unresolved feelings that have been lying dormant all these years."

Shelby snickered at such a suggestion. "Please. I don't live in the past."

Melanie shot her a look as if she didn't believe her. An unsettled emotion hit her in the belly, but she ignored it. "Lou's waving us forward. Here we go."

THE END WAS in sight as Josh continued to shake hands along the parade route. Only a hundred feet, and he'd be done with this portion of the day. Not that he'd minded working the crowd, but the heat of the day had left him sweaty and thirsty. He longed to go home, take a quick shower, then treat his dad to barbecued hamburgers and hot dogs at the Lions club.

After shaking the last hand, he walked the final few yards to the gazebo. "Josh, wait up!"

He turned to see the current mayor approaching him. "Mr. Mayor."

"I was hoping we could have a quick word."

Josh ran a hand along the back of his damp neck. "We can't talk at the Lions club?"

"I prefer more privacy."

Josh took note of the throng of people passing them. "Then why don't we set up an appointment at your office next week?"

"I can't show preference at this point to one candidate, Josh."

Was that what this was about? An endorsement from the current mayor for his campaign might have mixed results on his poll numbers, which Tim said needed major improvement. He was currently behind Shelby by double digits. And voters couldn't forget how Bill Conner had let them down. Still, he was the current mayor and probably had some sway in this town.

Bill took a step forward. "That is I can't publicly throw my support behind one candidate yet. But we both know that my support could certainly influence voters, and you definitely need it."

So why did this feel a little smarmy? "What are you asking for in return?"

Bill waved a hand. "Nothing major. Just a little assistance for a project close to my heart when the time comes."

The taste in his mouth soured. Was this what it would take to succeed in Thora's political realm? Currying favors and trading privileges to garner backing for initiatives that would benefit the town?

Still, without more details, he wouldn't rule out anything yet "I will take it under consideration when the time comes." That sounded neutral enough. "Now, if you'll excuse me, I've got to get home to my dad. See you around, Bill."

When he reached his car, Tim handed him a sweating bottle of cold water. "What was that all about?"

Josh drank deeply before answering. "Bill is looking for support on some kind of project if I get to be mayor."

"We could use his endorsement."

"I know, but at what price? And how much influence does the guy still have? A lot of voters remember his affair. It could hurt us in the long run." He wiped his mouth before tipping up the bottle again. "It's something to think about anyway."

"You don't want to upset the current mayor by refusing his backing."

"I'm not saying no. Not yet."

Tim eyed him and gave a nod. "Good. I'll meet you later at the Lion's club."

"I've been looking forward to a burnt hot dog all morning."

"You're there to do more than just eat. It's important that you talk to as many people as possible at the barbecue. We need to show everyone that you're approachable. That you listen to what they have to say."

"And I will. I want to, in fact. But I also want a hot dog with relish and a ton of mustard." Josh grinned as Tim rolled his eyes.

SHELBY SET HER large plastic container of cowboy caviar on the kitchen counter with the other side dishes, then walked out onto the back deck of Christopher's home. It had once belonged to her great-aunt Sarah, but she had sold it at the beginning of the year to her cousin's fiancé. Shelby had wondered if the family would splinter without having a home to gather at for holidays, but Christopher had opened it up for them, not just due to Penny. The family had adopted him and his kids without a blink of an eye. It's what Cuthberts did.

Penny waved, using her metal spatula. Three grills had been set up along the perimeter of the deck, and Shelby headed in her cousin's direction. Hamburger patties, wieners and bratwurst covered every available surface on the grills. Penny knocked her hip into Shelby's. "You're late, and you're always annoyingly early. Is everything okay?"

"The parade lasted a little longer than I expected is all, and I helped with cleaning up after." She adjusted the temperature on one of the grills that had started to burn the bratwurst. "What can I help you with?"

"It's all under control, so why don't you grab a cold drink and relax?"

"I'd rather stay busy."

Penny stared at her. "You're not worried about the debate tonight, are you? You've got this in the bag."

"I appreciate your vote of confidence, but this is turning out to be more challenging than I expected. Josh is gaining ground."

"He's got nothing to do but gain." Penny pointed to a semicircle of lawn chairs that had been placed under the large oak tree. "Hey, Aunt Sarah wanted to talk to you. Grab a couple of drinks and head on over to her."

Shelby nodded and pulled two cans of pop from a cooler and walked down the three deck steps to the lush green lawn. Aunt Sarah acknowledged her and pulled the closest empty chair to hers. "Shelby, take a seat."

Shelby handed her aunt a pop, then sat down, kicking off her sandals and letting her feet dangle into the grass. "Penny said you needed to talk."

"You looked great in the parade this morning."

"You were there?"

"They do let us out of the senior home on occasion, you know." Aunt Sarah gave her a grin when Shelby started to protest. "Relax. I'm teasing you."

"You're the second person to tell me to relax since I've gotten here."

"You need to do it more often, you know. But that's not what I wanted to chat about."

She paused and gazed at Shelby. "How is Josh Riley doing?"

"I still have a good lead on him, so everyone's saying that this is my election to lose. But he seems to be doing a lot of the right things, so I don't want to take my eye off the ball, so to speak." Why did she feel so unsure of the outcome?

"That's not what I meant, and you know it." Aunt Sarah blinked at her for long seconds. "How are the two of you getting along?"

"We're running against each other for an office we both want, so we're not *getting along*. We hate each other." She ran a hand through her hair, wishing she'd put it up so that it was off her neck in this humidity. "But the thing is, I don't think we do. At least, I don't hate him."

"And you're still attracted to him."

Shelby choked and pop arced out of her mouth. She wiped at the damp spot on her chest. "I am not attracted to Josh Riley." At least not enough to make it an issue.

Aunt Sarah crooked one eyebrow but didn't say a word as Shelby continued to make the wet stain on her T-shirt worse. Her aunt handed her a tissue that she brought out of her pocket, and she used it to mop at her mess. "Besides, that was years ago. And we both know how that turned out."

"Have I told you the story about my Henry?"

"Thousands of times. You met and fell in love before he was shipped out to Korea. You two fought because he didn't want to possibly leave you as a young widow, and you insisted it didn't matter because you loved him. You tried to work things out when he returned, but it didn't happen." Shelby scrubbed at the stain. "Did I get it right?"

"You got the basics, but you didn't say that I've never stopped loving him."

Shelby stopped scouring her top and looked at her aunt. "I never loved Josh. It was a schoolgirl crush. And I got over it real quick."

"But that attraction never stopped, right? Even now."

That was ridiculous. "I've grown up since then."

"So has he."

Shelby thought of him approaching her in

the parking lot. He'd seemed friendly. And he'd come to her rescue with the generator the day before. Maybe Aunt Sarah was right. He'd matured more than just physically. She swallowed at the warm feeling in her chest that started to spread, then dismissed it. "This is what you wanted to talk to me about?"

"No, but it's worth thinking over." Aunt Sarah settled in her chair. "I thought I'd set up a meet and greet for you at the seniors' home. I talked it over with Christopher, since he's the home's director, and he agreed. Of course, we'd also have to invite Josh to give him equal time and all that. What do you think?"

Shelby nodded. "Name the date and time, and I'll be there."

The afternoon continued in the lazy way that hot July days seemed to, and Shelby found herself relaxing. Almost forgetting about the debate later.

Almost.

Her family seemed to remind her of it with their questions and promises of support.

Was she prepared for the debate? Yes.

Could she beat Josh tonight? She was confident she could.

Would she win the election? Shelby had her doubts but didn't voice them. Instead, she gave her friends and family a big smile and insisted, "Of course I'm going to win. It's what we Cuthberts do."

During the annual volleyball game, she got called away by her sister, Laurel, who had just arrived. Shelby signaled for a time-out. When Uncle Mark groaned, she shrugged and headed to her sister.

Laurel was late, like always. Hadn't even shown up in enough time to eat. And she was way overdressed for a backyard barbecue, in a sleeveless silk blouse and skirt with heels. And she had that familiar look in her eye. Shelby slowed her steps. Her sister wanted something.

Laurel held the hand of her four-year-old daughter, Harper. Harper, in contrast to Laurel, had been dressed for the day in a navy tank top, sporting a sequined flag, and jean shorts. She tugged on her mom's hand. "Can I go play now?"

"Sure, baby." She leaned down and kissed

her, then straightened to greet Shelby. "I've been trying to call you for hours."

"I left my phone in the kitchen. What's going on?"

Laurel sighed. "Now, I know what you're going to tell me, but hear me out before you say no." She took a deep breath. "I have this great opportunity, but I have to leave right away to get to LA."

"You're going to California for a job?"

Laurel didn't answer her, and Shelby had a feeling that a man was involved. With her sister, a man was always involved. Shelby looked at Harper playing happily with her second cousins. "What are you doing with Harper?"

"I was hoping you'd take her. Just for a week or so."

"Laurel, I'm running for mayor on top of working full-time. What am I supposed to do with a four-year-old?"

"Maybe Mom will babysit when you need her."

Shelby narrowed her eyes. "Why didn't you ask Mom to take her?"

"I did, and she said no. She and Dad have plans to visit the McCormicks in Loughton this week." Laurel took Shelby's hand and squeezed it. "Please. Harper loves staying with you. Sometimes I think she likes living with you better than me."

"That's not true. She likes hanging out with me because I'm the aunt and get to spoil her rotten, which I love. You're the one with bedtimes and saying no to stuff." Shelby had to admit though, that Laurel's parenting style could occasionally be haphazard. She looked down at Laurel's hand still holding on to hers. "You've got to stop running away, Laurel. Are you really sure you're going to find anything better in California than you have here?" She looked up at her sister.

Laurel flung her hand away. "I came here to ask you for a favor, not to get a lecture. I'm doing just fine."

Shelby wondered if her sister was in some kind of trouble. The kind that maybe she didn't want to talk to the family about. She looked into her sister's eyes, but they were clear. "What about Harper? She needs her mother."

"Don't tell me what my daughter needs. Besides, you owe me." She tried to get

Harper's attention. "If you're not going to help me—"

"Wait." She really didn't need this right now, but what choice did she have? "She can stay with me."

Laurel's scowl softened into a smile. "See? Was that so hard?" She walked across the lawn to where Harper played, bent down, and hugged and kissed her daughter. Shelby followed her sister to a running car parked down the street. Shelby noted the ride-share sticker visible in the rear window. The driver rolled down the window. "If you want to make your flight, we have to leave now."

"We'll make it on time. Stop worrying." Laurel opened the back door of the vehicle and pulled out a Minnie Mouse backpack and handed it to Shelby. "I'll call you when I return." She smiled widely. "This could be a big thing for me. Huge."

Shelby clutched the backpack to her chest and watched as her sister got in and drove away. She turned, walked toward the house and entered the yard through a side gate. The volleyball game had resumed without her, which was fine since she didn't feel much like playing anymore. She approached her niece, who had donned a silk cape around her neck. "Look, Auntie Shel. I'm a superhero."

Shelby leaned down to get to the little girl's eye level. "I see that."

Harper glanced at the backpack in her arms, and her shoulders dropped. "I'm staying with you, aren't I?"

"What's the sad face for? You love visiting me."

The little girl shrugged and glanced away, but Shelby put a hand on her shoulder. "It's going to be fine, Harper. We always have fun."

"But my mom's not here."

Shelby pulled her into her arms and squeezed the girl. "It's okay. She'll be back."

JOSH CARRIED HIS plate of food to where his dad sat at one of the tables set up in the Lions club hall. The smell of the cooked hot dogs made his stomach rumble, and he was eager to bite into it before his nerves about the evening's debate increased.

As he passed the tables, he saw Mr. Hooks wave him over, and Josh heeded his old teacher's beckon. "Are you enjoying the barbecue, Mr. Hooks?"

"Sure am." He pulled out the empty chair next to him. "Sit. I've got a few people I'd like you to meet."

Not wanting to deny his old teacher anything, Josh took a seat and looked across the table at an older couple. Mr. Hooks introduced them as the principal of one of the elementary schools and a teacher at the high school. "Clare and Rodger have been working at the Thora schools for almost as long as you've been alive."

Josh whistled as he smiled at them. "I admire your dedication."

"Hal says that you've got ideas on how to improve the educational system in Thora," Clare said and folded her hands in front of her on the table. Josh assumed it was a pose she used when a wayward child had been directed to her office. "I'd love to hear what those ideas are."

Josh glanced at his hot dog and sighed. *Oh, well, the campaign had to come first.* "In your schools, you've seen hundreds of kids. Some succeed and are given a lot of attention. Then, you have those who act up and get a different kind of attention." Josh leaned forward. "My concern is for those kids who don't get seen. They're neither good nor bad. They're in the middle and often get lost in the crowd because they don't stand out noticeably. I know. I used to be one. Shuffled grade to grade without finding somewhere to belong. That is, until I learned that being bad got me the attention I craved. And I used that to my advantage."

"What are you suggesting exactly?" she asked.

"I'm talking about bringing passion back to a curriculum that has become too standardized, when all kids need to find their own way. Helping each student discover where they excel and supporting that rather than expecting them to do everything well."

"In other words, having different tracks for students." Rodger shook his head. "We tried that. It took a lot more teachers and resources, which meant more money out of a budget that is already so tight that it screams."

Josh held up his hand. "I get it. But what about volunteers who are experts in their fields and can work with kids?" Josh put a hand on Mr. Hooks's shoulder and nudged him. "If this man here hadn't turned my love of computers toward a positive outlet, I might have hacked my way into the wrong system and be watching life pass from the inside of a cell."

"Our volunteers are already stretched thin." Clare glanced at her husband before returning to him. "Josh, I admire your enthusiasm, but we've been teaching for a long time and seen ideas come and go about how to engage kids in the classroom."

"So tell me what you'd like to see. I'm always willing to listen."

THE CROWD AT the gazebo had doubled in the last ten minutes. Seemed everyone wanted to hear what the candidates had to say. Josh swallowed and turned his back on the crowd, closing his eyes and repeating the key phrases that would emphasize his platform. "Bring in more businesses. Reach out to corporations looking for that small-town feel. Bring back integrity to the office."

"And you think that's you?"

Josh opened his eyes and peered at Shelby. She looked polished in a red blouse with short white capris and sandals. Casual yet put together. And very patriotic. He reached up and adjusted the flag tie that Tim had handed him earlier. "The debate hasn't started yet."

She gave him a once-over. "The debate is always going. Every time you open your mouth, it's on."

He glanced at her mouth, noticing the red lipstick she'd applied. Without her braces that she had sported as a teen, she had a nice mouth. But then, he'd always noticed her smile, even with a mouth full of braces.

He played with his tie again, feeling as if it had tightened, cutting off his breath. "Maybe we should avoid talking to each other until the official debate begins."

"Sounds like a good plan to me."

She walked around to the other side of the gazebo. He watched her greet those who had set up their lawn chairs in the front row. She was so natural at this. What had he been thinking? There was no way he could win.

"Don't let her get to you," Tim said from beside him.

"I'm not." Well, that was a lie. He cleared

his throat. "Why is she not nervous? She acts as if she does this every day."

Tim took a step in front of him, looking him in the eyes. "Who cares? She's about to go down to defeat, and you're the man to take her there. Take a couple of deep breaths and get her out of your head."

But that was the thing. Shelby seemed to take a prominent spot in the front of his brain. The mayor introduced her to the crowd and she waved, claiming center stage in the gazebo. She exuded confidence. Poise. She looked and acted like the future mayor of Thora.

"And running against her is Joshua Riley, another Thora-homegrown candidate."

Tim nudged him, and Josh mounted the three steps up to the gazebo and nodded to the crowd. "Go, Josh!" someone in the back of the crowd shouted. A few people tittered, and he smiled. Shelby might act like the future mayor, but he wasn't going to give up without a fight.

The mayor introduced the moderators and reviewed the rules of the debate with the crowd. "Questions will be asked by myself, Chief of Police Scott Winter and city council member Karen Grime. The candidates will answer for five minutes, then have three minutes for rebuttal. Based on the toss of a coin, the first question will go to Ms. Cuthbert." The mayor turned to Shelby. "What in your history has prepared you for the office of mayor?"

Shelby stepped to the center of the gazebo and did a sweeping glance of the audience before speaking. "First, I'd like to thank you all for pausing your holiday activities to attend this debate. It does my heart good to see so many concerned citizens of Thora." She took a deep breath and clutched her hands in front of her chest. "I am also a concerned citizen of Thora and have been my whole life. The office of mayor requires a person of good reputation, which I have. It also requires a sense of public service. I've served on committees to beautify the park and improve the library. I've also held very successful fundraisers when the city's budget was too limited to pay for those and other improvements."

Josh watched her as she expounded on the ways she'd worked to help improve

Thora. If he wasn't running, he'd be marking his ballot for her.

But he was running against her, and he needed to bring his A game.

When Shelby finished speaking, she stepped back to give him center stage. He nodded at her, and then instead of standing in the gazebo, he strolled down the few steps so that he stood amid the crowd. He held out his arms. "Ms. Cuthbert brings up the point of reputation being an important part of being mayor. So let me ask, how many of you remember me from my youth?" Several hands shot up as a collective chuckle began near the back. "I get it. I wasn't exactly running committees and raising money for the town.

"Now, how many of you know what I've done since leaving Thora?" Hands dropped into laps, and the snickering ended. "Allow me to show you how reputation and service are very important in the office of mayor. And how I've changed in my time away and have succeeded at both."

JOSH WAS CONNECTING with folks in the crowd. He was good at it. Much better than her, if

Shelby wanted to be honest. She might have the facts and figures, but he had the charisma. He knew how to cut to the core of an issue and relate it to each person. Make them feel as if he was invested in what they were saying.

She noticed Melanie was listening to Josh with a rapt expression. Had her own campaign manager fallen under Josh's spell? Next to Mel stood Josh's campaign manager, scowling at Shelby. What had she ever done to Tim for him to dislike her? Her gaze landed back on Josh. He mounted the steps and reentered the gazebo. He winked at her before turning back to face the audience.

What was he winking at her for? And why had her heart sped up at that gesture? He may claim that he had changed, but he was still a big flirt. And she'd be wise to remember that winks and even his words couldn't be trusted. She'd fallen for them once, but not again.

The debate continued as they answered questions about their plans for Thora and how they'd balance the budget. Shelby thought she scored points on both of those topics since she had the numbers to back up her responses. Even the mayor seemed impressed.

Josh, on the other hand, scoffed at her suggestions. He depended on emotions rather than facts to drive home his message. Well, emotions got people only so far. She knew what she was talking about. Had always felt she'd understood what the town could use. That's what this debate was about, after all. Proving to her constituents that she was the best candidate.

She looked at the sea of faces that watched her. "How many of you remember going to get a cold pop at Stan's Grocery on a sultry night like this? But we can't do that anymore. Stan and his son, Leo, ran that store for more than three decades, until two years ago when the big grocery chain moved in. The mayor convinced us that it was a good thing to have it in our town. That it would bring in bigger tax revenues and lower prices for shoppers."

She paused and focused on one face in the crowd, like Melanie had coached her to. "But what did it do? Stan's couldn't compete with it and was forced to shut down.

Then the chain store declared bankruptcy and pulled out of Thora. Bringing in that big enterprise lost us tax revenues as well as a homegrown business. We lost jobs, and that building sits vacant on a prime lot. And now we have Josh Riley promoting the same thing as the mayor. He wants us to bring in the large chains to advance our economy, but we all know who loses in the end."

She turned to face Josh, whose smile had faded. "I, for one, want to see us win. To build local businesses up. Boost our jobs and our tax revenues. To improve our schools and city services." She directed her gaze back to the crowd. "And that's why voting for me is saying yes to a brighter future for Thora."

The applause bolstered her as she stepped back to give Josh the stage. He came forward and applauded, as well. "She's right. A vote for her will give us a future for Thora."

Shelby narrowed her eyes. This had to be a trick.

He shrugged. "We do need a boost to our jobs and economy. And we deserve improved city services and schools. But here's why Ms. Cuthbert's plan is shortsighted. The small businesses she wants to bring in won't generate enough money to fix the town's coffers. At least not enough to fund what she's proposing in the long term. But by attracting the bigger businesses, promoting our town for them to buy and build in, we can insure our future for long-term success."

When the crowd started to murmur, Josh quickly went on, "I know that losing Stan's Grocery was a blow to the community. But that's one instance. What about the larger stores that have opened here that we all go to and enjoy? What about the restaurants? The factories? Why can't we have both the small businesses and the nationwide chains to bring in more jobs and bigger dollars? Why is it either-or as Ms. Cuthbert seems to be saying? I'm open to all ideas to improve Thora because I understand that I don't know it all. I welcome and am interested in you and your ideas. And voting for me means that you will be heard."

Shelby frowned at his last words. When she'd been growing up, she'd had the title of Know-It-All and understood it wasn't meant as a compliment. While Josh wasn't calling her that, he seemed to imply it enough for her to bristle.

And what was so wrong with grasping what to do? Knowledge was power. But he made it sound like she would be a dictator. She was open to the suggestions of others and weighed them against what she knew. If their ideas were better, she conceded her own way.

Didn't she?

As Josh joined her at the back of the gazebo, the mayor stepped up to thank everyone for coming. "And if these fireworks weren't enough, we'll be having some more in about ten minutes. Enjoy your evening."

Shelby held out her hand to Josh. "Good debate."

He took it in his, running his thumb against the back of it. "I thought it went really well."

"And I'm not a know-it-all."

"I never said that." She tried to remove her hand from his, but he kept his grip on it.

"Let me go."

"I just want to talk to you for a minute."

"Why? So you can continue to tell me

everything I say is wrong?" She hated how the words came out so shrill. She cleared her throat. "I'll admit that you have some good ideas for Thora, but history has shown they won't work. Maybe you'd realize that if you had been around more."

This time, it was Josh who bristled, but at least he released her hand. She dropped it to her side and stared up into his eyes. The hurt in them reminded her of when he'd been younger and complained that he couldn't get a fair break from anyone in town. "I didn't mean…"

"I know what you meant. Have a good night." He gave her a nod and strode out of the gazebo, followed closely by Tim.

Shelby watched him as he stopped to talk to several people. What was it about him that made her lash out? She'd meant to compliment him and then leave. Instead, she'd found his vulnerable side and skewered it.

"You did great, Shelby." Melanie took the note cards from her hand and put them in her pocket. "You stuck to your talking points and emphasized the pillars of your platform, just like we practiced."

Shelby glanced at her. "Then why do I feel like Josh did better?"

Melanie gave a shrug. "He didn't do better, but he did hold his own. He had some good points, which we could explore in order to see how we can improve on your platform."

"Do I come across as too superior? Unapproachable?" Shelby rubbed her bare arms. "Don't answer that. A recent conversation with Laurel tells me I am." She looked out to the crowd. People were getting settled for a better view of the fireworks. "I've got to find my parents. They have Harper with them, and I need to get her home and in bed."

"Are you going to be able to take care of her on top of everything else?"

"Of course."

She walked down the few steps from the gazebo and shook hands with people as she made her way. Her family had staked a claim on a corner closest to the street, their usual spot for viewing the fireworks. Shelby found her mom sitting in a lawn chair, Harper sleeping in her lap. "I'm going to take her home."

"Don't you want to stay for the show?"

"I had enough fireworks during the debate." She lifted Harper from her mother's embrace and held the child's head to her shoulder. "Thanks for watching her."

Her mother stood and handed Shelby the backpack, hooking it over her free arm. "You have to stop giving in to your sister's demands. She'll keep expecting you to do things for her if you don't. There's a difference between helping out and being taken advantage of."

"I know."

"And yet you still do it."

"I'm thinking of Harper, Mom." She shifted the weight of her niece. "I'll call you in the morning, okay?"

Shelby carried the child to her Mustang. History had taught her to have a car seat ready at all times. As she was getting Harper buckled in, she heard her name being called. Josh jogged up to her. "You're leaving before the fireworks?"

"It's been a long day." She shut the door and looked into his eyes. "About what I said earlier about you not being around…"

Josh waved it off. "It's fine."

"No, it's not. You seem to bring out the worst in me, and I say things without thinking. I'll work on it, promise. Even if you are my enemy."

"I don't want to be your enemy, Shelby."

She reached up and pushed a strand of hair out of her eyes, but a warm breeze blew it forward again. Josh caught the strand and tucked it behind her ear. The gesture made her heart flutter. Biting her lip, she glanced at his mouth before shaking her head. "Anyways, I hope you enjoy the rest of your evening."

He pointed to her back seat. "I didn't know you had a daughter."

"She's my sister Laurel's little girl, but she's staying with me for a few days."

"You're always helping someone out. I used to admire that about you."

"Used to?"

"Still do. You have a big heart, and it's obvious that you care a lot about your family and this town."

He took a step toward her, and she found herself tipping her head back to look into his face. Behind him, a burst of red lights followed by yellow and green flashed in the night sky, accompanied by a loud boom. "You're missing the fireworks," she told him.

He kept his gaze on hers as more fireworks flashed and sounded. "I'm not missing a thing." He reached up and touched her ear where he'd tucked in her hair. "Shelby, when did you get to be this beautiful, inside and out?"

"Auntie Shel, it's too loud!" Harper cried from the back seat.

Shelby took a step back from Josh. "I gotta go." She opened her driver's door, but looked at him one more time, the fireworks lighting up his face in reds, blues, yellows. "I'm pitching at the softball game tomorrow."

"Are you asking me to go with you?"

She shook her head, finding the idea ridiculous. "No, I'm telling you that you might want to make an appearance too. It's one of the newer Founders Week events, and it's a prime time to get in front of the voters."

"Oh." He almost sounded disappointed, and why did that make her heart beat faster?

"It was just an idea."

He said goodbye, turned on his heel and caught up to a group staring at the lit sky. Shelby watched him for a moment and wondered why she'd given her opponent such good campaign advice.

CHAPTER FOUR

THE THORA POLICE DEPARTMENT trailed the
Thora Fire Department by two runs in the
last inning of the softball game. Shelby had
been able to keep the police to only four
hits, but her arm ached and she'd given up
two of those hits in that inning. Tim was
up to bat with runners on first and third.
Penny, playing catcher, gave her the signal
for a fastball. Shelby shook it off. She didn't
know if she had enough strength to put any
fire behind it.

Penny frowned at her and gave the fastball signal again. Shelby smacked the softball into her glove. Her gaze settled on
the police bench and found Josh watching
her. She liked that he'd listened to her, and
they'd both done some hand shaking and
small talk among the spectators before the
game started. People were starting to warm

up to him, which was good for his campaign.

She shook her head again at Penny, who changed up the signal to a curveball. One nod from Shelby, and she wound up to give the pitch.

Tim bunted the ball, and it dropped a few feet in front of her. She scrambled to retrieve it and fired it at Penny to keep the runner on third base.

"Two outs!" the umpire called and swept the dirt off the plate.

"Time-out," Penny said and approached the mound. She tilted up the catcher's cage to peer at Shelby and shielded her eyes from the sun with one hand. "You have enough to finish this game?"

Shelby nodded. "Just one more out. I got this."

"I really want to take the trophy home this year since it's my first time on the team, okay?"

"No problem."

Penny returned to home plate, and the umpire restarted the game. Instead of Lou heading off the bench to bat, however, Josh approached the plate. "Last-minute substitution," he told the umpire.

Shelby frowned at the change and threw the ball into her mitt several times while she waited on the mound. Josh took a few practice swings, then got into his stance. Penny gave the signal for a fastball, but Shelby shook it off because she suspected he anticipated that call. The signal changed to high and inside. Shelby gave a nod and fired the ball at the plate.

"Strike one."

Josh took a step back, swung the bat and reentered the batter's box. Penny repeated the high-and-inside signal, and Shelby threw the ball with a little more force than the last pitch. Josh tried to hit it, but it bounced off his bat and stayed to the left of the third-base line.

"Foul ball. Strike two."

Penny tossed the ball back to her, and Shelby caught it easily. One more pitch, and she could end this game. Her gaze was drawn to Josh's face, his expression indicating he seemed to be enjoying this a little too much. She ignored Penny's signal and threw a pitch to brush him back.

"Ball one."

Josh smiled at her, gave her a wink, and she brushed him back again, just to show that she could.

"Ball two."

Penny threw the ball back with a glare, and Shelby smacked the ball against her mitt a few times. She couldn't let him get to her. She had enough juice for one more fastball, so when Penny gave the signal for it, she nodded. The pitch left her hand in a straight line for the catcher's mitt, but Josh hit it toward the outfield. The center fielder caught it easily, ending the game.

Josh changed his direction from trotting to first to approaching her on the mound. "You're really good. I forgot you were on the high school team."

"My parents wanted us to be well-rounded in athletics as well as academics." She peered at him. "You almost had that last hit."

"I haven't done that in years, but it seems that Thora keeps its teams going."

Shelby nodded at the players gathered along the baseline. "And its rivalries." She held out her hand to him. "Good game."

He took her hand in his and tugged her a little closer to him. "But you're thinking you've beaten me, right?"

This time, she was the one to wink at him. She joined the fire department's team as the players moved through the line, slapping the hands of their opponents. Tim brought over the shiny trophy and handed it to Penny who hoisted it over her head to the cheers of her teammates.

Once they'd all returned to their respective dugouts, Josh went to the pitcher's mound. Shelby changed from her cleats into tennis shoes and wondered what that man was up to now.

He cupped his hands around his mouth to amplify his voice. "Thanks to both teams for playing a great game. And let's keep up the celebration with cold drinks provided by the person who would like to be your next mayor."

Tim and another cop carried two large coolers out to the field, and the fans from the stands soon surrounded them to get a bottle of water or pop. Shelby smacked her knee. She should have thought of that. After sitting in the hot sun for a few hours, everyone would be thirsty. Penny put a hand on her arm. "You'll get them next time."

"We won the game."

Penny gestured at the crowd around Josh. "You know what I mean."

JOSH SHOOK ANOTHER hand and strained to see over the heads of all the people to find Shelby, but she seemed to have disappeared. Instead, he came face-to-face with her cousin Penny, who accepted a bottle of pop from him. "Smart idea to have beverages for after the game."

He smiled at the petite woman who looked a lot like Shelby with her blue eyes. "I thought so."

"You'll have to be even smarter to beat Shelby for mayor though." She opened her drink and took a long swig.

He glanced around again to see if he could find his rival. "Did she leave already?"

Penny nodded and walked away while Josh wished that he'd asked Shelby to stay after the game. *And do what, Riley?* It's not like she wanted to spend time with him.

But last night during the fireworks, he'd

sensed a spark between them. The good kind. If he'd had more courage, he would have kissed her while the night-sky show illuminated her creamy skin in reds and blues. He'd wanted to, but had chickened out.

Not to mention, he shouldn't be thinking about kissing Shelby or wanting to talk to her or anything else right now. She was his opponent in this race, and only one of them could win.

"Brilliant move with the cold drinks, man," Tim said. "People will remember this when they vote next month."

"Maybe." He turned to his campaign manager. "I think I need to show up to more of these things. With Founders Week, there's something going on every day, so we need to be more proactive. What's tomorrow?"

"Classic Car Night at Ted's Diner."

Josh smiled brightly. Shelby would be sure to be there with her souped-up car. "Perfect."

"Are you serious about doing more of this stuff? Because I can get you invited to all these events." Tim brought out his cell phone. "I'm going to make some calls. Put things in motion." He held up his cell phone. "Do you have a suit you could wear?"

"A suit for what?"

But Tim had already walked away, jabbering to someone on his phone. Josh continued to hand out more bottles of water and pop until everyone had left the ball field. He stacked the near-empty coolers on top of each other and carried them to his truck.

Back at home, he paused outside the living room window and heard the drone of the television. He'd left the old man in his recliner, and it sounded like that's exactly where he'd stayed. Wondering if things would ever change, Josh unlocked the back door and entered the house through the kitchen. He put his keys in the bowl on the counter, debating whether he should try to talk to his dad. He decided instead to avoid a fight and went to his bedroom and turned on the light. He was in the middle of working on a new baseball app that he hoped would fund the coming year for him.

After several hours of playing with the code, his head throbbed and his back ached from hunching over his computer. A soft knock broke his concentration. The bedroom door creaked open, and his dad stood there. "I didn't hear you come in."

"You were too involved in your show."

His dad's expression didn't change. "I've got a doctor's appointment tomorrow morning. You said you'd take me."

"I said I would, and I will." He faced the computer monitor. If he could just figure out this one section, the whole program would fall into place.

"Well… Good night."

His dad closed the door, and Josh turned to look at it. Would it ever get easier between them? Setting aside his concern, Josh returned to his work, telling himself he'd try to sort out his relationship with his dad tomorrow. For now, solving a confusing bunch of code seemed the easier problem to concentrate on.

SHELBY RUBBED THE hood of her Shelby Mustang with a chamois and stopped to check what looked like a dent. She should have left the car at the garage overnight instead of at her condo complex, but she hadn't planned on a thunderstorm early that morning.

The Carson family were heading into Ted's Diner just as the Jorgensons were leaving. They all wished Shelby well and she returned the greeting.

A whistle from behind her stopped her short, and she turned to find Josh standing there, grinning. "That's some car."

She polished an already-polished spot on the hood. "Did you want something?"

His eyes danced as he walked toward her, but then he swerved to run a hand along the roof of the Mustang. "You must have put a lot of time and money into this restoration."

"Enough."

"You give it a name too?"

It suddenly seemed silly to her, but she nodded. "I call it Starry Night."

"After the van Gogh painting?"

She raised an eyebrow at him. "I figured you forgot everything after graduating high school. Guess I was wrong. But then, it seems that I'm discovering new things about you every day."

"Like what?"

"Like you have a passion for kids and their education. Didn't see that one coming."

He stepped closer to her, athough pivoted

around her so that he stood closer to the car. "Tim tells me that you're judging the talent show tomorrow night."

"They asked me months ago."

He smiled at her. "They asked me this morning, so I guess we'll both be sitting at the judges' table."

She shouldn't be surprised by the news, but she still found it hard to breathe. Seemed like everywhere she went lately, Josh was there. Granted, it had been her suggestion for the softball game yesterday, but now he was at the car show tonight? And the talent show tomorrow night. She supposed he'd finagled an invitation to the library fundraiser on Friday too. Well, she would do her best to avoid him there.

And yet she found herself looking forward to spending time with him. There was a lot about him that she didn't know but wanted to. She groaned and held her head in her hands.

"Are you okay?"

"The sun must be getting to me. I was actually thinking that I might be starting to like you."

This time, he did step up to her and stayed

there. He seemed to be searching her eyes. "And would that be such a horrible thing?"

"You're my rival, so yes."

"We can like each other and still be running for the same office."

"You like me too?"

Josh hesitated. "Maybe respect is a better word."

She regarded him for a long moment. "The truth is, I might have been wrong about you."

"Might have been?"

"Okay, I was wrong. You have changed from the rapscallion I recall."

"Ooh, rapscallion, huh? I feel like one of those bad boys in the Regency romance novels you used to read during study hall, when you were supposed to be finishing schoolwork."

"I didn't look at them until after my homework was done." She cocked her head to one side. "You remember that?"

"You'd be surprised at what I can remember."

"But you couldn't remember to take me to prom, could you? Or was it that you didn't want to go with me, after all?" She regretted the words as soon as she'd spoken them. She hadn't meant to bring up old history after admitting he'd changed. But there it was. It was out now.

Josh winced. "I'm sorry. I was stupid and made a lot of bad choices then, and that was one of them. I should have shown up."

She closed her eyes and rubbed her forehead. "It was years ago."

He placed a gentle hand on her arm. "I didn't mean to hurt you."

She stepped back far enough so that his hand fell to his side. "It's old news. And we've both gotten past it, right?"

And she had. She'd outgrown her silly crush on him. Hadn't she?

He watched her for a long while. "I should go check out the other cars."

She gave him a stiff nod, but kept an eye on him as he held up a hand in farewell and walked on to the next car. But he didn't stop to talk to the owner like he had with her. Instead, he kept walking and she regretted that he'd left.

JOSH ADJUSTED THE blazer that Tim had insisted he wear to act as judge of the talent show. The high school auditorium's central air unit seemed to be malfunctioning, because the air was warm and stale. A bead of sweat started to fall from his brow, and he lifted his hand to wipe it away.

It had to be the heat and not the fact that he'd be seeing Shelby again. The second she had mentioned him standing her up for prom, he'd known that he'd made a bigger mistake than he'd realized back then. He might have been a bad boy in high school, but he hadn't played with the emotions of girls. He always told them upfront that he wasn't boyfriend material. His dad would have been even more disappointed in him than he already was if that hadn't been the case.

He was the person most disappointed in himself that he had let Shelby down. To be honest, he'd never expected her to agree to go with him when he'd mentioned the dance. But she had. And then he hadn't shown up that night. Instead, he had spent the evening hacking into the school's computer system to see if he could, and he'd completely forgotten about prom and Shelby and everything else.

He wiped his forehead again as an authoritative-looking woman with a pile of papers approached him. "Good, you're here already. Sorry about the AC. Link's on the roof, checking out the unit now."

He gave her a nod and tried to recall her name. She'd been a year or two behind him at Thora High. Jenn or Jill or Jane?

"Good evening, Jess. It's a hot one to-night, isn't it?" Shelby said as she fanned herself with the program for the evening's show.

That was it. Jessica. He thought she might have been in choir or drama. Maybe both. He tended to black out his memories from that time. He hadn't done much to be proud of. Better to focus on how far he'd come since then.

"Link said give him twenty minutes, and the air should be back on," Jessica relayed. "I'm so glad you both agreed to be judges tonight. You wouldn't believe how hard it is to get volunteers for these things."

Shelby nodded, her fan moving faster. "Believe me. I know. I've tried for years to get enough volunteers for the blood drive and the tree planting." She made a noise in the back of her throat. "Unless it involves free food, it's like pulling teeth."

"I never thought to offer refreshments to the judges, but I'll jot that down for next year. That might get me more help. Thanks, Shelby."

Jessica made a note on her papers and left them standing at the front of the auditorium. Josh looked Shelby over. She'd dressed in a sleeveless dress in a soft peach that matched her complexion. She looked sweet enough to taste. He closed his eyes briefly, wondering where that thought had come from. "You look nice tonight."

She stopped fanning herself and gave him a once-over. "Thank you. You look… hot." At her words, she waved a hand in front of her face. "I didn't mean you look hot as in good-looking. I meant, it's warm in here."

He felt a smile start to form on his face as he watched her get so flustered. "I knew what you were saying."

She gave a short nod and continued to try to cool herself with the program. "Hopefully, this heat won't keep people away. It'd be a shame after all the practice these acts have put into it if they didn't have a decent-sized audience."

"I have to admit that I've never gone to the talent show. What can I expect?" He figured if he could get her talking, then she'd get comfortable with him again. He didn't like to see her this uptight. He longed for the easy conversation they'd had before.

She sighed. "There's some singers. Usually a garage band or two. Maybe a dance troupe. Mostly musical acts. Although, one year, Mr. Bassett did a recitation from Shakespeare, and he was pretty good."

"I've never judged something like this either."

She shrugged, then glanced away. "It's mostly a matter of personal taste. Did the act perform well? Did they have stage presence? Things like that."

"You've judged these before." He said it as a statement because he could tell it was true.

"Jessica knows she can depend on me."

He winced at her words. "Listen, Shelby, about prom night…"

She waved her hand between them. "Ancient history, okay? It doesn't matter any-more."

"But you're right when you said that I've changed. I'm not that guy who would hurt you. I hope we can be friends again."

She tipped her head to one side. "Have we ever been friends?"

"Well, friendly, at least. In fact, I was wondering if I could take you to the carni-val tomorrow night." Her eyes widened, and her mouth opened, gaping at him and his in-vitation. Had he made her speechless? Mark the date on the calendar. "Just as friends."

She started to say something, but they were interrupted by Jessica. "I'm about to let the audience in, so I need you both to take your spots at the judges' table."

Shelby nodded and led him onto the stage where a table with two chairs had been placed to the side. She pulled out the folding chair and sat down, handing him a sheet that listed the performances, as well as a pen. "You're going to score each act from one to five, with one being the best. And we'll con-fer after the show to determine the winner."

"You didn't give me an answer about the carnival."

She looked at him, and he had a moment of panic. She was going to turn him down, wasn't she? Probably for the best, since they were campaigning against each other. "Never mind. It was a stupid idea."

"No, actually, I'd like to go with you."

He perused her face to see if she was joking. Instead, she appeared to be serious. "Why?"

"But we'll have to bring my niece with us."

He felt himself nodding in agreement. "Sure. I'll pick you both up at seven?"

"Make it six. We can avoid the longer lines if we get there during dinnertime. We'll eat early."

Further conversation about their plans ended as the talent show began. Josh scored the different acts and marveled that he'd scored a date with Shelby Cuthbert. And that he was truly looking forward to it.

Maybe it wasn't a *date*. Maybe it was more them becoming friends. Like he'd suggested. Political rivals could be friends, couldn't they?

In the end, the Poison cover band won the talent show, but Josh felt as if he'd won too, as Shelby placed a slip of paper in his hand. "My condo's address. See you at six."

THE SMELL OF corn dogs and deep-fried cookies never failed to boost Shelby's spirits. She held Harper's hand as they walked through the carnival, past the different food stations and toward the ticket booth. When she started to open her purse to buy the tickets, Josh waved off her money. "This one's on me."

Harper clapped her hands as they entered the line for the carousel. "When I grow up, I'm going to have four ponies."

Shelby laughed and put a hand on her niece's back to guide her through the ropes to the front of the line. "Four, huh? And what will you do with all of them?"

"Ride them, of course. But they're going to be real so I can brush their hair and put bows in their mane. And I'll name them things like Sunshine and Rainbow and Stormy and Thunder."

"Good names," Josh told her. "Have you ever ridden a real pony?"

Harper hung her head, looking at the

ground. "Mama says it's too 'spensive. But one day, I'll have all the money so I can."

Harper led them to several merry-go-round horses before deciding on a gray one that had a bright purple saddle with a yellow star. "This one, definitely."

Shelby leaned down to pick up the girl and set her astride the horse, then belted her in before choosing the one next to hers. Josh picked the horse on the other side of Shelby. "I can't remember the last time I rode on a carousel. If I ever did."

"Did you and your family come here for the carnival?"

"We used to, before my brother died." He shrugged. "My parents gave up on a lot of family outings after that."

Shelby studied Josh and would have offered her condolences, but he'd said it so matter-of-factly. No emotion. Nothing. Instead, she reached over and put her hand on his. His gaze turned to her, and she offered him a smile, which he slowly returned.

The merry-go-round started to turn, and Harper let out a yowl worthy of a bonafide cowboy. Shelby echoed it, and Josh added his to the mix.

After the carousel, they walked past the faster rides. Shelby had never been fond of them, and having Harper with them gave her the perfect out. Josh stopped in front of the fun house. She started to back away, but he grabbed her hand. "Oh, come on. It's not too scary." He turned to Harper. "You want to go in, don't you?"

Harper looked up at Shelby and tugged on her other hand. "Please. Can we go?"

Shelby scowled at Josh. "No fair recruiting my niece against me." She gave a shiver. "Fine, we'll go. But we all stay together."

Josh leaned closer to her and squeezed her hand. "Don't worry. I'll protect you if you get too scared."

Shelby wondered briefly who would protect her from him.

Josh handed over the tickets to the teenage boy collecting them at the front. He ushered them inside the fun house, and Harper gasped when the door shut behind them with a loud thwack. "Auntie Shel—"

Shelby let go of Josh's hand and leaned down in front of the four-year-old. "It's okay. We'll be safe."

Josh stooped and picked the little girl up.

"How about I hold on to you just in case you get frightened?"

Harper nodded, and they moved to the next room that had several trick mirrors. In one, Josh and Harper had long foreheads and small, squat bodies. Shelby giggled at the image and stood in front of another that stretched her into a thin beanpole. Josh took her hand and pulled her into the next room. It was dark, and there came a sound like someone breathing heavy. Harper hid her face in Josh's shoulder as Shelby clung to his arm. "Nothing will get you in here, Shelby."

Still, she held on to him until they moved into the following room, which had unstable footing. It felt as if they were walking along gelatin to get to the next area where they found a pit of plastic balls instead of a floor. Josh set Harper down. She reached in and flung the balls in the air. "C'mon, Auntie Shel. You do it too."

She let go of Josh's arm and picked up several balls to toss them in the air. Her niece clapped and looked at Josh. "You too, Mr. Josh."

"You throw them for me."

"Okay, but it's a lot of fun!" She threw a few, then ran back to him. "Pick me up."

Josh did as she'd asked and put her over his shoulders as they waded through the balls into the next room. To get to the other side, they had to crawl through a padded tube that turned on a spindle. Harper attempted it first but kept falling onto her knees and then spinning around. Shelby followed her, helping her niece to get to the other side. They stood and waited, hand in hand, for Josh to join them. Like Harper, he kept dropping to his knees and then tumbling with the tube rather than making forward progress. He looked up at Shelby. "Help."

She grinned as she crawled back into the tube. "Don't plant your knees so hard into the surface. That's what makes you fall."

She held one of his hands and pulled him forward. "This way."

He kept his eyes on hers as they inched toward the end of the tube. They were near the finish when Josh slipped and pulled Shelby down, where they whirled around. They laughed as they finally made it out, holding hands. Harper giggled with them and took Josh's other hand as they entered a room that appeared to be the exit. So they strode forward until a clown jumped out from behind a barrel. Shelby screamed along with Harper, and they both turned and clung to Josh.

"We're almost there," he told them softly. "You guys can do this."

Shelby took a deep breath and peeked over her shoulder at the metal door. They were only steps away from it. She turned but kept a tight grip on Josh's arm as they reached the exit and pushed through. The stomach-rumbling scent of the carnival greeted them. Shelby turned to Harper. "It's okay, sweetie. We made it."

Harper opened one eye and looked at her, but she wouldn't move. Josh picked up her niece and carried her out of the fun house. "See? That wasn't so bad." He rubbed Harper's back. "And I think my two brave girls deserve an ice cream."

Harper lifted her head and nodded. "I like ice cream."

Josh had called them his girls. Shelby

paused for a minute at that until she realized they were watching her. "Make mine chocolate."

AFTER EATING ICE CREAM, they rode the carousel again, then Josh suggested the Ferris wheel. Shelby looked up at the tall ride and seemed to pale. "You're not afraid of heights, are you?"

"N-no." She looked to where the line snaked along the bottom of the ride. "But there's a long wait. Don't you think we should ride something else?"

Josh put his arm around her shoulders. "You'll be fine. I'll protect you, just like I did in the fun house."

They entered the line, and Harper chatted about the Founders Week picnic planned for that Saturday. "Granny's making bunches and bunches of 'tato salad for it." She peered up at Josh. "Do you like 'tato salad?"

"A little, but I prefer to eat other stuff more."

"Like what?"

"Hot dogs. Chips. And Old Sammy's chili." He turned to Shelby. "Does he still make it for the picnic?"

"Old Sammy died a few years ago, but his son makes it now. It's good but not quite the same."

So many changes had taken place while he'd been in Pennsylvania. Deaths. Births. Graduations. Anniversaries. Good times and not so good times. People had moved out while others moved in. And then, there were changes like the woman beside him. She had grown up into a real beauty. Sure, she was bossy, but that didn't change the way her blue eyes lit up when she was talking to her niece. Or the way she'd clung to him in the fun house.

The line moved up a little more, and Shelby glanced at the Ferris wheel. "I don't know if I can go on this."

"Have you ever been on it before?"

"Junior high. Labor Day–weekend carnival." She shuddered at the memory. "I'd had too many root beers and curly fries, and my cousin Jack kept rocking the cart until I got sick."

"That won't happen this time."

She looked up at him, her blue eyes wide and unsure. "It's not the height that scares me. It's how the cart rocks back and forth."

"We'll keep it steady, Freddy. Okay?"

She nodded but looked up again at the wheel. "Calm as water on a pond."

"Still as a corpse."

She winced. "Bad choice of words."

He laughed and pulled her closer to his side. He enjoyed spending time with this version of Shelby. One who wasn't so controlled and strict. "Trust me, Shelby."

"I get into trouble when I do," she said but followed him onto the Ferris wheel seat when it was their turn.

He placed Harper between them and put his arm across the back of the cart, one hand on Shelby's bare shoulder. The wheel started to turn, and Shelby clung to the metal edge, squeezing her eyes shut. "Tell me when it's over."

"So, Old Sammy died. What else has changed since I've been gone?"

She opened one eye and peered at him. "Are you trying to distract me?"

He gave a shrug and rubbed her shoulder. "Humor me."

She closed her eyes and sighed. "My nana died at the beginning of last year. It's been hard on the family without her. She was like the center of everything we did, and now that she's gone, we seem to be drifting apart. I guess that's why I try to keep up her traditions. So we don't lose that closeness. Before she died, I promised that I would do what was best for the family."

"You Cuthberts are a tight clan."

She nodded and squealed as the wheel moved higher. "Family is important."

"To you anyway." He looked out toward the rooftops of the houses that surrounded the park. His own place wasn't that far away. He'd left his father in front of the television before picking up Shelby and Harper. That was something that hadn't changed since he'd first left Thora. "Sometimes I wonder why I moved back here."

"To take care of your father."

He found that she'd turned to him with her eyes open. "Not that it seems to matter to him. I bet he'd actually prefer it if I left."

"Don't say that. He's your father."

"Not every family is like yours, Shelby. Not all of us grew up living a charmed life full of trips to the carnival and big holiday parties." He let one of his fingers caress her shoulder. "You probably won't believe me, but I was jealous of you back in high school."

"Of me? You called me *brainiac* and *metal mouth*. And you made fun of my bad eyesight." She tilted her head to one side. "You were the one who was popular, even if you were getting into trouble all the time."

"But you had family who showed up for your graduation. Who filled the auditorium with hoots and hollers after you gave the valedictory speech."

"You had a date any night you wanted one. And so many friends that you were never alone. They always surrounded you when you walked down the halls at school."

"You knew what you wanted and went after it."

"You…" She hesitated. "I was jealous of you too. You could do anything, and no one stopped you. I had to follow the rules."

"Admit it. You like the rules."

A faint smile played around her lips as she shrugged. "I find it easier to live inside those barriers. But sometimes…" She shifted and focused on the west where the sun hung low on the horizon. "I'd like to forget the rules and try the impossible."

"You took over your dad's garage. I'd say that's pretty close. Amazing, in fact." When she started to look away, he shook her shoulder. "What dreams do you have, Shelby?"

She stared at Harper, who had fallen asleep, squeezed to his side. "I have responsibilities. Not dreams."

"But if you could, what impossible thing would you do?"

The wheel rotated slowly as the passengers left and others filled the seats. Shelby clutched the metal railing across their lap, and he thought she wasn't going to answer him. But then she asked, "What was it like to leave Thora behind?"

The question surprised him. He'd thought she'd be the type that would live and die in their hometown, while he was the type to always leave. He remembered when he'd boarded the bus that had taken him to Pittsburgh the morning after graduation. "Like being released from prison." She glanced at him, and he shrugged. "I knew that if I stayed here, I'd always be that Josh Riley. The juvenile delinquent. The one who sprayed graffiti on the senior rock. I'd never be able to escape that reputation." He sighed.

"Pittsburgh gave me a second chance. And I made the most of it."

"So now you've returned to the prison and want to be its mayor. Why?"

"Let me ask you. Why are you running for mayor of a town you really want to leave?"

"I didn't say I wanted to leave."

Josh reached out and touched her cheek. "You didn't have to."

Josh drove them back to Shelby's condo and carried the sleeping Harper inside. Shelby led him to the guest room where the little girl evidently stayed, then pulled down the sheet and quilt so he could lay her on the bed. He stood back in the doorway as she removed the girl's sandals, then drew the bedding over Harper, who turned on her side and curled her fist under her chin. Shelby leaned down and kissed the girl's forehead and turned off the light beside the bed.

Shelby tiptoed out of the bedroom and left the door open an inch. Josh followed her to the living room. He glanced around the space and gave a nod. "This is how I expected you'd decorate."

"Are you calling me predictable?"

He took a few steps toward her, but she backed away. Her phone, stuck in the pocket of her jean capris, started to ring. She held up one finger to Josh, then answered after noticing Melanie's name. "Did you pick up the flyers from the printer today?"

"Did you go to the carnival with Josh Riley tonight?"

Word sure had traveled fast. "Nothing happened."

"Except the whole town saw the two of you on the Ferris wheel."

Shelby turned her back on Josh and dropped the volume of her voice. "I can't really talk right now."

"He's there, isn't he? Shelby Cuthbert, what is going on in that head of yours? He is the enemy."

"No, he's not." If she'd learned anything during that evening, it was that Josh Riley was not her foe and could become her friend. Even a good one, if she let him. "Can we talk later?"

"Walk him to the door and tell him good-night, then call me right back."

Shelby turned back to Josh. "That was Melanie."

"She probably wasn't too happy that we were hanging out."

"No, she wasn't." Shelby suddenly felt sad. "But she was right about one thing. You should probably go."

He nodded, but didn't move. Just stood there in her living room and stared at her with a look in his eyes that she had once longed to see when she was a teenager. The air heated between them until he let out a long breath. "Good night, then."

She followed him to the door, but before he walked out, he abruptly faced her. She wondered if he was going to kiss her, but he kept her at arm's length. "I had a really good time with you, and I think you enjoyed it too. Don't let Melanie change your mind about that."

Then he pivoted and left. Shelby stood in the doorway and watched him stride along the sidewalk. She waited until she heard his truck start before she shut the door and rested the back of her head against it. Sighing, she pushed herself off and collapsed onto her couch.

When she returned Melanie's call, it went

straight to voice mail, so she wasn't surprised at the knock on her door moments later. "What were you thinking?" her friend asked as she brushed past her and headed directly to the kitchen.

Shelby smiled when Mel plunked down a bakery box onto her kitchen table. "You're angry with me, but you stopped to pick up a dessert to share?"

"I bought it for me." She opened the lid and pulled out a cherry pie that had been sold at the carnival along with other baked goods to raise money to build a barrier-free playground. Shelby had made and donated two batches of brownies for it. "But I'll let you have some if you get us some plates."

Shelby opened a cupboard and pulled out two small plates and a couple of forks before joining Mel. "Is it just the two of us, or did you also invite Jack to come over and harangue me?"

"Just us." Melanie had found a knife and had started to slice into the pie. "I figured I could get the whole truth out of you without him here. So spill. What were you doing with Josh Riley?"

"Did everyone also tell you that we had Harper with us the whole time? We were babysitting."

"Why did you go to the carnival with him in the first place?"

"Because he asked me." But that wasn't the whole reason. She'd been surprised by his invitation, and even more by her acceptance. She'd wanted to get to know him. Not as her rival but as a man. To see how he measured up to her memory of the boy he'd once been.

And she'd discovered that he was so much more.

He'd stirred things up inside her that no one ever had. Had she really admitted that she longed to leave Thora? Maybe not in so many words, but he'd reached a part of her that she'd been so good at hiding from everyone else.

Why are you running for mayor of a town you want to leave? It was a worthy question she was afraid to explore too closely.

Melanie placed a piece of pie in front of Shelby. "People are wondering why the two of you were together. They're thinking that you approve of Josh and his plans."

Shelby lifted her eyes to meet Melanie's concerned gaze. "We never talked politics."

"What did you talk about, then?"

"Nothing."

Melanie's skeptical expression was obvious. "You expect me to believe that you spent a couple of hours together, and you didn't talk?"

"We talked, but it wasn't about anything important." But it had been. He'd given her a glimpse of who he truly was, and she'd done the same. "It's no big deal."

"Shelby, this is a very big deal. You're running against him, so no more of this. Stay away from him unless it's a debate or the town hall meeting on Saturday."

Shelby knew that she was right again. But part of her wanted to call Josh after Melanie left. To see if the connection she'd felt with him had been mutual. To appease Mel, she gave a single nod of her head.

Her friend and campaign manager seemed to calm at her acquiescence, but Shelby felt stirred up. Unlike how she'd been in a long time. Something had chipped away part of her defenses and she wondered if it was her time to explore these feelings she had for Josh.

Because she could no longer deny that they were still there, waiting for her to give them a chance.

Even if this was the worst possible time for them.

CHAPTER FIVE

"STAY AWAY FROM SHELBY."

Josh was shocked at his campaign manager's admonition. In his estimation, the closer he got to Shelby, the better his poll numbers would get. She was the town sweetheart, so what could it hurt to be friendly with her?

You've got no business messing with her, his dad had said when he'd returned from the carnival last night.

The thing was that he wasn't messing with her. If anything, being with her was messing with his own mind. He'd confessed things to her on the Ferris wheel that he'd never shared with another person. And he knew he'd seen past her carefully constructed armor. She'd shown him a glimpse of the real Shelby, and he'd been drawn to that vulnerable side of her.

Now as he circulated around the library fundraising event, he wondered when she'd show. He found himself glancing at the entrance doors of the library every few minutes. But no Shelby yet. Would she approach him or should he go to her? Because despite Tim's warnings to stay away from her, he needed to talk with her.

Had she felt it too? That something indefinable that drew him to her? That connected them on a deeper level?

He closed his eyes and tried to shake that off. Best to mingle and try to drum up more support for his campaign. Not moon over the woman who could thwart his goal.

While circulating around the room, he introduced himself to a group of people.

One of the women looked him over with obvious interest. She thrust out a hand. "You probably don't remember me. I used to be Alyssa Winfield."

He searched her face and nodded. They'd been out a few times in high school, but it had never been anything serious. "I should have known. What have you been up to, Alyssa?"

"Getting divorced."

"Sorry to hear that."

She laughed and put a hand on his bicep.

"I'm not." She flipped her long brown hair over one shoulder. "We had some good times back in the day."

He could tell she was hoping they could continue them in the present day, but he moved on to the next group of people. While he was talking about his plan to use the abandoned factories and retail spaces in order to attract big businesses, the air warmed. He glanced at the entrance to find Shelby entering with her campaign manager in tow. Her eyes found his across the room, and his heart seemed to stop beating until she gave him a nod and glided to a different section of the library.

"What businesses are you approaching to come here?" Mrs. Johnson asked. He recognized her from the same street that his dad lived on.

He tried to focus on her, unsure of what he'd been saying. *Get your head back in the campaign, Riley.* "Um, I have a contact with a Pittsburgh manufacturing company that is looking to expand in the Midwest. Bringing them to Thora would create some much-needed jobs. And that means good news for all of us."

He saw Shelby looking through the clipboards that listed items in the silent auction. He thanked his audience for their time and then walked toward her. She wore a gauzy dress in a shimmery blue that matched the color of her eyes. "Find something good to bid on?"

She looked up at him and blinked before dropping her gaze back to the clipboard and signing her name with a flourish. "Maybe."

He read the item and whistled. "A private chef making dinner for two. I didn't realize that you were into French cuisine?"

"I've always wanted to see Paris." She glanced to one side of him and then the other. "I shouldn't be talking to you."

"Me either."

She placed the pen back on the clipboard and started to walk away. He reached out and grabbed her hand. "Wait."

"I shouldn't have gone to the carnival with you. And now I think it's best that we stay away from each other."

"But you don't want to." He raised a brow.

"Doesn't matter what I want." She scanned the room. "We both need to focus on our campaigns right now."

"You're right."

She stared at him, and everything in his periphery vision seemed to fade. All he could see was her. All he wanted was her.

Then she took a deep breath and moved on.

After she left, he bid on the French dinner, adding a couple hundred dollars. If he won, he could invite her to join him. She would have to talk to him then.

SHELBY MADE THE rounds of the fundraiser but seemed to find Josh in her line of vision no matter where she looked. And he looked really good. He'd worn a linen blazer in a light shade of gray with a blue button-down shirt that might have matched the color of her own dress. He'd shaved since last night, and his bare cheeks and upper lip made his boyish looks more innocent.

She had to stop thinking about Josh. Melanie was right that she had to focus on winning her campaign. She had to be mayor. Everyone expected her to win.

Jack handed her a glass of white wine and followed her gaze to where Josh stood with a pair of town council members. "He seems to have them interested in whatever he's saying."

She took a sip and shrugged. "Who is that?"

"Come on, you've been staring at him since you walked in." He waved his fingers in front of her face. "What's going on?"

"Nothing."

"My mom saw you at the carnival with him. Said you two looked pretty chummy."

Shelby rolled her eyes, then took another drink. "People need to find something else to talk about. It was no big deal."

Melanie joined them, carrying a plate of crudités. "She talking about Josh? Again?"

"Is there something going on between you two?"

"No." But she understood it for the lie it was. "I'm going to check my bids in the silent auction."

When she looked at the French dinner, she saw that several people including Josh had bid more than her. She bit her lip, considering her budget. What the heck. A larger bid would mean more computers and materials for the library. She picked up the pen and wrote a larger figure on the clipboard, hoping that no one else would try to beat it.

"You really want that French dinner, don't you?"

She didn't have to look up to know that Josh had cornered her again. "It's for a good cause."

"Why Paris?"

"Why not? I've never traveled outside of the US. But to be honest, it's Greece that I've been dreaming about lately."

"For the beaches?"

"For the history." She gave a shrug. "And the beaches. I've checked out books from here to plan a trip."

"And when are you taking that vacation?"

Shelby didn't answer but moved to the next clipboard for a pontoon boat. The thought of it made her stomach grow light and nauseous. Pass. Ooh, a makeover. She wouldn't mind that, especially once she was mayor and running town hall meetings. Her cousin Kristine had let her borrow the dress she wore and had made recommendations of how to accessorize it. She signed her name on the clipboard and put a modest dollar amount following it.

Josh stepped closer and took the next clipboard. "Suite at a Detroit Tigers game including a catered meal. Yes, please." He held it out to her. "Or were you going to bid on this one?"

She took it and signed her name before handing it back. "Why are you interested in a French meal?"

"I've been cooking for my dad the last few months, so it might be nice to have someone else do the honors for a change." He put his name on the Detroit Tigers package. "If I win, you'll have to join me. I don't know if I've ever had a French dinner."

She huffed. "What part of 'it's best that we stay away from each other' did you not understand?"

"Oh, I understood. And I agree that we should. But I'm also choosing to ignore the suggestion."

"It wasn't a suggestion." She turned and saw that several people were watching them. She dropped the tone of her voice to a whisper. "I don't know what game you're trying to play, but I won't be a part of it."

"Who says it's a game?"

She saw the sincerity shining in his eyes,

but she couldn't do this. Not now. Maybe after the election she could explore whatever this was. But at that moment, she had to walk away.

Before she did, she grabbed the clipboard for the French chef and wrote a larger figure by her name. It would mean eating peanut-butter-and-jelly sandwiches for a month, but it would be worth it.

She left but glanced over her shoulder to find Josh bidding on the same dinner. He winked at her, then went to join a group that included the library director.

Stalking back to the clipboard, she read the figure he'd written and paled. He'd added a zero at the end of the last bid. Melanie joined her and looked at the clipboard. "What are you doing?"

"I need to borrow some money."

Melanie held up her hands. "Don't be looking at me for that much."

"I can't let him win." She bit her lip and tried to calculate how much she could afford and knew that it wasn't enough.

"Then don't you think it's time you stop whatever this is between you and Josh and refocus on what's important here. Let him have the French dinner, but don't give him the election." Melanie took the clipboard from Shelby's hands. "Bring that rivalry to the town meeting tomorrow night. If you give even an inch, he will exploit it until it's a mile."

"He's not like that."

"Are you sure?" Melanie raised an eyebrow at her. "Don't fall for this act of his. If he can get you off track, he can steal this election from under you." She gripped Shelby's elbow. "This is your election to lose. Don't you dare give him a single voter, Shelby."

"Fine. He can have the dinner." She picked another clipboard and made a larger bid and signed her name with a flourish. "I'll take the ball game."

THE THREAT OF rain and thunder hung over the town picnic as citizens gathered at the park with their portable grills and lawn chairs. The gazebo had several tables laden with different dishes that folks had brought, and everything was served potluck-style.

Josh moved along the line with a paper plate that was already heavy. He joined his dad at the selection of desserts and stayed his hand from cutting a large piece of cherry pie. "Dad. Your diabetes."

"I took my medicine."

"As well as a brownie and a scoop of… What is that? Pink fluff?"

"Ambrosia salad. It's got fruit, so it's good for you."

"I see Doc over there by the grills. Should I go double-check with him?"

His dad scowled and flung the pie server onto the table. "Fine. You're as bad as your mother."

Josh only hoped he was as good at taking care of him as she had been. Instead, he felt like it was a losing battle every meal. His dad's plate didn't have a single vegetable on it. He glanced at his own and shrugged. He hadn't done much better.

They took their seats near Tim's family under one of the large oak trees. Glancing around, he hoped he'd catch a glimpse of Shelby. He'd seen a congregation of Cuthberts on the other side of the gazebo, but not her. This was a prime campaign opportunity, so he knew she would be there.

"Do you have your speech prepared for later?" Tim asked as he dug into some ribs.

Josh patted the chest pocket of his collared shirt. "It's a mix of jokes and serious plans for revitalizing Thora. I've got this."

His old man chuckled. "What you've got is a long shot of beating Shelby. Why not stop wasting everyone's time and bow out with grace now?"

"My poll numbers are going up, Dad. People are listening to me."

His dad made a face but didn't say another word. Maybe he was right. He couldn't even convince his own father that he was the best candidate to be mayor.

Tim gave him a pointed look. "You're going to win this election. And usher in a new era of prosperity for Thora."

He hoped so.

After the picnic ended, the leftovers were packaged up and the tables removed from the gazebo. People pulled their lawn chairs closer to hear the speeches. First, the library director gave a short lesson about the founders of Thora, then the mayor talked about all he'd accomplished in his eight years in office. A council member spoke about the things that were in motion currently in the town. At the end of her speech, she asked for both mayoral candidates to join her at the gazebo.

Josh rose from his chair and saw that Shelby had been in the center of the large gang of Cuthberts. She turned to face him, and he gave her a soft nod. He held out his hand to help her up the step to the gazebo, and a rumble of thunder interrupted them. Several people glanced up at the darkening sky but stayed in their seats.

Shelby looked into his eyes, and he waved at her to start the speeches. She produced a stack of cards and flipped through them before addressing the crowd. "Citizens of Thora, we are on the precipice of change. You have two candidates who want what's best for our town but propose very different ways of achieving it.

"I believe that we need to bolster our small businesses. That we can't depend on a big corporation to sweep in and save us. We have always depended on doing the hard work ourselves. From the first days of Thora— when my three-times-great-grandfather and -grandmother moved here to make a better life for their family—to now, when we have a community of almost twenty thousand who want that same thing. We want to make a better life for our families. And that's what I want for Thora. To make us better. Stronger. And ready to face the future with hope and promise."

She stepped back to polite applause. He put a hand on her shoulder and smiled to her before taking the spot she'd just left. He kept his notes in his pocket since he knew the speech by heart. But jokes and platitudes weren't what Thora needed right now.

Tim stood near the back of the crowd, moving his hand in a motion to get started. Josh cleared his throat. "Shelby is right about wanting a better future for Thora and that we have different plans of how to do just that. I know that the businesses and the families we've lost the last couple of years have hurt us. And I understand that we want to hold on to hope and promises. But we deserve something more."

He took the few steps down to the first row of chairs and pointed to one of the guys he'd graduated with. "Hank, you deserve to know that the factory is going to reopen and hire you, so you can provide for your family." He moved to someone else. "Mrs. Horton, you have the right to know that the taxes you pay are being used responsibly so that when you need medical assistance, an ambulance will be available."

He looked out into the crowd and felt a raindrop fall on his cheek. "Dad, you deserve a mayor who will listen to you when you talk about what worked in the past. And, Tim, you deserve a police force that is well equipped to handle the calls you're sent on."

He mounted the steps back up to the gazebo. "We can't pin our hopes on campaign promises. We all need to roll up our sleeves and get back to work to make Thora better. Because it's going to take more than just the mayor to make it better. It's going to take all of us doing our part. Doing the hard work required to make our town better. If we come together, the sum of our efforts will be worth it."

At his last words, the rain that had held off for most of the afternoon began in earnest. Most people grabbed their lawn chairs and ran to the parking lot for the refuge of their cars. Others crowded into the gazebo.

Josh found himself pressed against Shelby as more people tried to escape the rain. She backed away, but more people pushed her closer against him.

Josh felt a little silly, but he had to admit that he enjoyed having her close to him. To look down on the part in her hair. And the way she looked up at him. "Sorry," she whispered as she tried to move so that space would open between them.

Someone shuffled by and she came flush against him. She stumbled a little and he reached around to put his hand on her back. "I don't mind."

She kept her eyes on his, and he thought about kissing her and seeing if his curiosity about her would be quenched. But showing that kind of affection in the middle of all these people was exactly what Tim had been warning him against. So instead, he enjoyed the chance he had to hold her in his arms.

The rain continued, and more people started to dash away to their cars, alleviating the tight quarters. Shelby took a step away, and he missed her body against his.

Soon, only a handful of people remained

in the gazebo. Shelby leaned against one of the railings and looked toward the path. "I suppose that I should make a run for my car. There won't be any more speeches now."

He let his gaze follow the curve of her shoulder, from her arm to her elegant fingers that gripped the railing. When she turned to face him, he gave a nod, though he couldn't be sure what else she'd been saying. Something about tomorrow. He glanced among the folks that remained in the park but didn't see his dad. Why hadn't he thought of him earlier? "I wonder where my dad took off to."

"I saw Tim take him to his car."

"Good. He shouldn't be out in the rain like this."

There was a flash of lightning followed by a rumble of thunder. Shelby wrapped her arms around her middle. "I should go."

"Shelby…" She paused to look at him, and he took the few steps to reach her. "I enjoyed your speech."

A smile flirted with her lips. "And here I thought yours was better."

"Founders Week is over, so I guess I won't be seeing you at any more events."

She shrugged. "I guess not. That's too bad. I was starting to enjoy our time together."

That surprised him since she had insisted that they stay away from each other just the night before. He wondered what it was that she really wanted. He reached out and took her hand. "Shelby, are you saying that you want us to see each other?"

She looked up at him for a long moment without saying anything, then gave a shake of her head. "No. That would be the worst thing for both of our campaigns. It would send confusing messages to the voters, and that's something that neither one of us wants. But I did enjoy spending this week with you."

"You did?"

"Didn't you?"

He nodded. "More than I expected." He continued to look into her eyes. "I'm not saying we should date, but I don't see the problem with being in each other's company. I won that French dinner at the auction last night. Maybe you'd like to—"

"Josh, I don't know what I was thinking. Maybe after the election we can be friends, but it's important that I win. I'll see you around town," she said, waving. "Good luck on election day."

"You too."

Then she turned and ran to the parking lot. He looked up at the sky. It didn't seem like this storm was going to end anytime soon. He sighed before dashing toward his truck. No sign of his dad or Tim's car. He got inside and pulled out his cell phone to text Tim. Sure enough, his campaign manager had taken his dad home. He tapped out a thanks, then started his engine. The windshield wipers parted the rain, revealing Shelby sitting inside her car a few spots away from his. She hit her steering wheel with the butt of her hand and leaned down. Could be she was having engine trouble.

He shut off his truck and braced himself for the downpour before opening his door and running to hers. He bent down, resting his arm on the roof of the Mustang, and knocked on the window. She jumped and spotted him before rolling her window down a crack. "What's the problem?" he asked her.

"Won't start." She turned the key in the ignition, but the engine didn't growl to life.

"Pop your hood."

"I was going to wait the rain out before I checked."

He looked up at the dark clouds above them. "It's not going to stop anytime soon. Pop it."

She pulled the lever to release the lock on the hood and he walked to the front of the car. The engine looked cleaner than most kitchens he'd seen, but then, he knew that Shelby had always put her heart into restoring the car. He checked the fluid levels, but they were full. The battery leads were tight, but the battery itself looked as if it had seen better days.

"I knew I should have checked the battery before I left for the picnic," Shelby said at his shoulder and leaned across to put her hand on it. "It's been giving me problems, but I figured I had enough power for the day."

"You should be inside the car, staying dry."

She looked down at her blouse and pulled

the wet material from her chest. "I'm already drenched. I won't melt."

Josh wiped off the moisture that had gathered on his forehead and dripped down his nose. "I could give you a jump."

"That's okay, I'll call one of my cousins to come and do it."

"Shelby, I'm already here. And I'm not going to leave you stranded in the parking lot while you wait for someone else to help you. Let me."

She nodded, and he touched her shoulder before sprinting to his truck. He parked it so that they were nose to nose. He grabbed his jumper cables and hooked them first on her car, then his. Shelby turned the key, but nothing. Josh got into his truck and pressed the accelerator to rev his engine and send the power to her car. She groaned after the second try yielded no results. They waited until trying a third time, but still zilch.

Josh shut down his truck and ran to her window. "Any other ideas?"

"Nothing. I'm going to have to call Eddie for a tow, but it could be a while before he gets here."

"I'll wait with you."

He returned to his truck as she phoned on her cell. After the call, she darted to his truck and opened his passenger-side door. "You mind if I sit in here with you where it's warm? Eddie said he can be here in about half an hour."

"Get in. Where's Harper?"

"My parents took her to their house when the speeches started." She got settled in the truck while he ramped up the heater to help them dry off. Their wet skin and clothes made them shiver, and Shelby held her hands up to one of the warm vents. "This is not how I expected the day to go."

He grinned at her words. "Most of my days don't go as planned."

"Mine do. And I tend to get testy when they don't."

"What in your life hasn't gone to plan? You lead the most charmed life of any person I know."

"Plenty of things."

He placed his arm along the bench seat and turned to look at her. "Name one."

"When I was in high school, I figured that I'd have my own business."

"Which you do."

"And I'd be married with at least one kid by now. That hasn't happened."

"Why haven't you gotten married?"

"Came close once, but looking back on it now he was all wrong for me. Called me controlling and boring when it was more due to the fact that he couldn't commit to one woman." She gave a shrug. "What about you?"

"Why didn't I get married?" He chuckled. "You should know that I'm not the marrying type."

"Oh, please. If the right woman came along, you'd marry her in a second."

"Then, maybe she hasn't showed up yet."

Silence fell as they looked at each other. Shelby faced forward and rubbed her arms vigorously. "You don't have a blanket or something in the truck, do you? I'm freezing."

"We could use each other's body heat to warm up." She gave him a look that said she couldn't believe he'd make such a suggestion. He held up his hands in surrender. "Suit yourself."

They sat in silence for a moment. He reached over and put the radio on to give them something to fill the quiet. A song that had been popular when they were in high school started playing, and he lowered the volume. "Man, this piece brings back some memories. Still, I wouldn't go back to those days."

"Can I ask you something, and you'll give me an honest answer?"

Immediately, he wondered what she would want to know. "Shoot."

"Did you do all the things they said you did in high school?"

He'd been accused of a lot of stuff back in the day but had been guilty of only some. "Like what?"

"Skipping school to see superhero movies on their first day?"

He nodded. "Busted. But I wasn't the only one."

"Did you really egg the principal's house on Halloween our senior year?"

He winced at that one. "Not my best moment, I'll admit. But he'd been riding me since the first day of school, and it felt like a tiny way of giving it back to him."

"Did you make out with a teacher in the teachers' lounge?"

"Partly true." When Shelby turned to look at him with raised eyebrows, he shrugged and fought to keep from blushing. "It was in the janitor's closet, and it wasn't a teacher. Angela was a year behind us in school."

Shelby shook her head at this. "Did you graffiti the senior rock?"

He wanted to evade that question, but he'd promised to give an honest answer. Painting the large rock near the football field and signing the names of the year's graduating seniors on it had been a tradition for years. During the spring of their senior year, someone had spray painted obscenities over the rock. "I said I did, didn't I?"

"That's the thing though. I always felt as if you were covering up for somebody else." She narrowed her eyes at him and clicked on the overhead light. "I was studying at the library that night and I saw you, so there's no way you could have done it."

"I could have, after the library closed."

"But you walked south in the direction of your house. The school is to the east."

"I veered off course. No big deal."

"But where did you get the spray paint?"

"In my backpack."

"I saw what was in your backpack when you put your books away at the library. There were no paint cans." She stared at him. "You said you'd give me an honest answer."

"Shelby, don't push me on this one. I can't give you what you want."

Another song from their high school days started to play, this one slow and full of the memories of teenage yearnings. "About prom night…"

She looked up at him, the overhead light making shadows of her eyelashes on her cheeks like two dark half-moons. "You don't owe me anything. It's done and over."

"I really did want to go with you that night."

Her mouth dropped open, and her voice came out soft. "You did?"

"And if I had, I would have danced all night to this song with you."

Shelby kept her eyes on him. "Don't say things you don't mean."

"I do mean it. I think you were one of the few people in this town that talked to me as if I mattered." He reached over and brushed one wet strand of hair from her cheek. "You still are."

She turned so that she faced him. "Melanie says that I shouldn't be seen with you. That being with you endorses your campaign."

"And what do you think?"

She didn't answer for a long moment, and he thought she was going to change the subject, then she took a deep breath. "I think that there's something between us. And it scares me at the same time that it makes me want to sing along with that song."

"I feel it too. This pull toward you that I can't escape."

"I don't want to escape."

"Then don't."

And he pressed his mouth against hers. She couldn't stop smiling, and when he backed away, she said, "Wait. I can do better than that."

And she brought her mouth to his, letting her kisses say what she couldn't.

CHAPTER SIX

HER CELL PHONE kept ringing, but Shelby wanted a few more minutes of slumber. After Eddie had towed the Mustang to the garage and she'd picked up her other car to retrieve Harper from her parents' house, it was late. Besides, she'd replayed her kisses with Josh while they'd waited in his truck so often that sleep had been the last thing she wanted.

Groaning, she flipped over on her stomach and reached across to the nightstand to grab her phone. "Have you seen this morning's newspaper?" It was her mom.

"Good morning to you too, Mother."

"What were you thinking, Shelby Brianne?"

Uh-oh. She'd been called by her middle name too. Never a good sign. "I don't know. What's in the paper?"

"A picture of you and Josh. Kissing."

Shelby closed her eyes. "How did the paper get a picture of that?"

"You didn't answer my question. What were you thinking by kissing Josh Riley?"

She hadn't been thinking for once. Instead, she'd let herself be in the moment and enjoy his kisses. And there'd been a lot to enjoy. But they'd been parked in his truck during the thunderstorm. Who would have seen them? Much less taken their picture? "It's nothing, Mom."

But everything between her and Josh had been building to that instant. And she hadn't been disappointed. It had far surpassed what she had fantasized in high school. She sighed at last night's memory.

"Are you planning on seeing him again?"

No, that was not happening. In fact, by the time Eddie had arrived with the tow truck, she and Josh had come to their senses.

Even if she had programmed his phone number into hers. And had texted him once she had gotten home, at his request to know that she was safe.

"It's not a good idea, Shelby. You've got too much riding on this election to be dating your opponent."

"We're not dating."

Even though she wasn't sure what they were doing at this point. Maybe they would both realize that it had been a mistake. Even if a part of her wished it would happen again.

Her mom sighed on the other end of the phone. "Good. I'd hate for you to get involved with that man."

"That man? Mom, he's changed from the boy we all remember. Did you know he was named Pittsburgh's citizen of the year?"

Her mom gasped. "It's worse than I suspected. You're defending him."

"No, I'm simply stating that you should give him a chance. He really is a good man."

"Not when he's running against my daughter, he's not."

Shelby knew kissing Josh had been a mistake, but it had been a delicious one. Even now in the light of day, she touched her lips which seemed to burn with memory. "You don't have anything to worry about, Mom. It won't happen again."

"The real reason I called was about Laurel."

"She's still in California, right?"

"Your father is on his way to pick her up

from the airport as we speak. Seems things didn't work out like she'd hoped."

"That's too bad."

"You're a good sister with a level head on your shoulders. Don't let this mistake with Josh change the path you've worked so hard to take."

Her phone continually rang while Shelby bathed Harper. With her hands full of bubbles and her phone ringing in the other room, she let the call go to voice mail. "Okay, kiddo. Time to get dressed. Your mama will be here soon."

Harper splashed her hands in the water and lifted her palms full of bubbles. "Can I wear the new sundress that you got me? With the red sandals?"

"Absolutely."

Once Harper was dressed in her new outfit and ensconced on her sofa, staring out the front window for signs of her mother, Shelby retrieved her phone. Twelve missed calls? She checked her voice mail to find seven messages, two of them from Melanie and one from Josh. What had been said in the newspaper?

She opened her front door and retrieved

the paper from her porch. Unfolding it, she sighed at the headline below the picture of her and Josh that graced the front page above the fold. *Mayoral candidates swap more than ideas the night of the Founders Week speeches.* Ugh. Drew really needed to get a better editor.

Certain words popped out as she perused the article. *Rumor. Gossip. Bringing dishonor to an esteemed election.* At least Drew had been evenhanded with his portrayal of both Josh and her. He'd disparaged them equally and questioned their motives.

Shelby collapsed onto the armchair near the sofa and continued reading. When she finished, she tossed the newspaper aside but then rose to her feet and picked it up from the floor to put in the recycling bin. Just because she seemed to have torpedoed her election chances didn't give her the right to make a mess of her home too.

"She's here! She's here!" Harper jumped up and down on the sofa, then hopped off to race to the front door, opening it before Laurel had gotten out of her car. Harper ran to her mother, who scooped her up in her arms and rained kisses on her cheeks.

Shelby joined them outside by Laurel's car. "How was California?"

Her sister eyed her and hugged her daughter tightly. "Did you miss me, Harpie? I got you a present. Go get your stuff, and we'll go home so you can see it."

Harper cheered and wiggled out of her mother's arms to run back into the house. Laurel leaned on her car. "Was she any trouble?"

"She never is."

"She's got a new outfit, I see. From you or Mom?"

"Does it matter? She's already outgrowing the clothes you packed for her."

Laurel narrowed her eyes. "Don't tell me how to take care of my daughter."

"That's the problem. Lately, you haven't been taking care of her. You've been depending on me and Mom and Dad to do it for you." Shelby peered at her sister, who had a telltale flush on her cheeks. "Are you drunk right now?"

She waved off the suggestion. "I made myself a mimosa after Daddy dropped me off at home. No big deal."

Shelby wondered how big of a drink. "It

is when you're driving with your daughter in the car." She held out her hand. "Give me your keys. I'm not going to let you set off in this condition."

"It was one drink, Shel. I'm fine." But Shelby kept her hand held out until Laurel dropped the keys into her palm. "Whatever. You're so uptight. I suppose you'll be the one transporting us home?"

The way she asked made Shelby think of the car accident, but she put it from her mind. "Is everything okay? Because you haven't seemed yourself lately."

"California didn't turn out like I'd hoped, but I'll be fine." She smiled as Harper ran toward them. "We'll be fine."

Harper joined them at the car, dragging her backpack behind her. Laurel put a hand on her damp curls. "Auntie Shel is going to drive us home, baby. Won't that be fun? I'll sit in the back with you and we can pretend we're rich and she's our chauffeur."

THE FRONT-PAGE PICTURE of Thora's Sunday paper brought several calls to Josh's cell phone but not the one he'd been hoping for.

"So, what was it like kissing Shelby?" Tim asked him.

It had been heaven.

And inevitable. And now that he'd had a taste, he wanted more, unfortunately. "Why do you want to know?"

"Because we've all wondered about Miss Ice Princess."

"Don't call her that."

Tim chuckled on the other end of the phone. "She got to you, didn't she? Well, I need you to get your head back in the game. Getting cozy with Shelby might have gotten you a few more voters, but we need a lot more than the romantics in this town to vote you into office."

"I didn't kiss her to get votes."

"Then why did you do it?"

Not wanting to answer that question, Josh posed one of his own. "When is the meeting with Cosart? I think we need to come up with a solid proposal for bringing his factory to Thora. One that he can't turn down."

"You don't kiss and tell. Is that it?"

"Tim…"

"Fine."

They spent the next several minutes plotting out how to entice Cosart's business to Thora, with Josh taking notes. When he hung up with Tim, he checked his phone to see if Shelby had called him back.

Nothing.

He rose from the kitchen table to pour himself another cup of coffee and found his father watching him from the doorway. He raised the half-full carafe. "Need a refill?"

His dad held out his empty mug. "You were serious about bringing that Cosart fellow here."

"I really think it would help the town. Bring in jobs. Be security for families. It could be a huge game changer for Thora." He replaced the carafe after filling his own mug and taking a sip. "What do you think?"

His dad started, as if surprised to be asked for his opinion. He took a few steps into the kitchen and cocked his head to one side. "I think you're right."

Josh gave a soft chuckle. "Well, mark this day on the calendar. You agreed with me on something."

"Don't let it go to your head." His old man started to shuffle out of the kitchen but turned back. "And don't be playing with the emotions of a good lady like Shelby."

"It was just a kiss."

"Smart, caring women like Shelby put a lot of meaning into them." Then he turned and left the room.

Josh leaned against the counter while he considered his father's words. Shelby probably did put a lot of significance behind her kisses. But the truth was he did too, when it came to her. The passion that had stirred up between them inside his truck had rocked him. Made him question what it was he really wanted. Because he couldn't have both Shelby and the election. It was one or the other. He'd lain awake until the early hours of the morning, debating his choices.

If he chose Shelby, he might have love and a relationship, things that he'd started to crave in the last few years as his career success pointed out the empty spaces in his life. He could see that path with her likely leading to marriage and a family. Or to heartache, if things didn't go the way he hoped.

On the other hand, if he chose the election, he could win the town's respect, including his father's. Maybe even earn his love. And wasn't that why he'd returned to Thora in the first place?

He set his mug on the table and grabbed his phone. This time she answered. "I need to see you," he told her. "But somewhere that won't have a hundred eyes watching us."

ON THAT LAZY summer Sunday afternoon, Shelby met Josh at the busy outlet mall. "This isn't what I meant when I talked about meeting somewhere private."

"If someone wants to catch us together, I doubt they'll drive an hour away to do it." She looked at him across the general-info counter. Glad to have something separating them so that she didn't jump into his arms and see if the magic from the night before had been a fleeting thing. "Let's go."

They strolled along, their arms at their sides. Once in a while, his hand would brush hers, sending tingles along her skin that had nothing to do with the air-conditioning. But he didn't hold her hand, as much as she might want him to. And she didn't take his, because this conversation would be better if they weren't touching. Finally, she said what they were both thinking, "What happened last night, the kissing, can't happen again."

She became aware that Josh had stopped and turned to find him watching her. She walked toward him. "That's what you were going to say, weren't you? Because you're right. We can't do that again."

He gave a nod, but it seemed to be given reluctantly. When he started walking again, he brushed past her and she had to hurry to catch up to his long strides. "Could you slow down?"

He stopped near a young family, the mother wiping the chocolate ice cream—smeared mouth of a little boy while the father held the hand of a toddler who waited to get his own mouth cleaned. Shelby smiled before turning to Josh, who had a lost look in his eyes. She reached out to take his hand, hoping that it might bring him comfort.

He pulled her into his arms and buried his head into her hair. She wanted to kiss him. She wanted to run away. She wanted to cry. But she swallowed all of that down and closed her eyes, putting a hand on the back of his neck and stroking.

Finally, Josh stepped back but still held on to her hand. They moved, not talking or looking at each other. She knew that this was a moment that they wouldn't have again once they left the mall and went their separate ways. She didn't want their closeness to end.

Not yet.

They made a circuit around the mall while she wondered what he was thinking. If he hurt as much as she did. This chance they were throwing away might never come back around. But they needed to be apart from each other and keep their eyes on the election.

They stopped in front of the water fountain, and Josh reached into his pocket and brought out a couple of coins. He closed his eyes for a moment, then tossed one into the water to join the others that rested on the bottom. He handed the last to her. "Make a wish."

The coin seemed to burn her palm as she closed her eyes. *I wish I didn't have to choose between Josh and the election.*

She tossed the coin, and it plopped into the water and joined Josh's.

"If all we get is this afternoon, I don't want to leave you yet." He squeezed her hand. "Can you stay?"

She had a list of things that waited at home for her to complete, but they didn't seem to matter more than the man standing in front of her. "What do you have in mind?"

JOSH HANDED SHELBY her ice cream cone before he bent down to join her where she sat on the sand, staring out at the lake. He gave a quick lick of his strawberry-cheesecake scoop before it dripped down his hand. "I missed being so close to the Great Lakes when I was in Pittsburgh. I had a condo on the riverfront, but it's not the same as sitting on the beach like this."

"It's what I'd miss most if I ever left."

He turned to look at her. "So why don't you leave? What's keeping you here?"

She looked like she wanted to explain, but licked her cone instead. He momentarily forgot his own ice cream as he watched her. She could be so distracting, without even trying. Which was why they could have only this afternoon together.

They finished their treats and stared out at the boats that dotted the surface of the lake, the lull of a Sunday afternoon making him drowsy.

Finally, Shelby asked, "Do you ever go back to a decision where you turned right and ask yourself what would have happened if you'd turned left instead? That a different choice could have taken you down a path that might have been better?"

"Don't we all?" He leaned closer to her so their shoulders touched. "What was yours?"

"That's just it. I didn't really have a choice. And if I had to relive that moment, I'd do the same thing all over again and be in this same exact spot." She buried her face into her hands.

He put his arm around her shoulders and pulled her to him, resting his chin on the top of her head. "You can tell me, Shelby."

She put a hand on his chest. "I don't want to ruin this afternoon by talking about it."

"We're getting to know each other, so it won't ruin a thing." He held her tight and she relaxed inside his arms. "You're safe here."

"You mean that, don't you?" She sighed and seemed to sink further into him. "My sister, Laurel, called me one night and asked me to pick her up from a party where she'd been drinking. I didn't want her driving since it had been sleeting out, and the roads were a mess."

"Was this recent?"

"No. I was a sophomore in college, and Laurel was a senior in high school." Shelby raised her head to look at him. "I couldn't leave her there, and I couldn't let her drive either."

"Of course."

Shelby again rested on his chest. "I was about two blocks from home when the car hit some ice and spun out of control. The car behind us hit our passenger side, crushing the door against my sister. She broke her pelvis and leg and had to have several surgeries. The doctor prescribed strong pain medication to help her. It took a while to get her off the pills. But I'm worried that now… she may have started taking them again or maybe something else. She hasn't been herself lately, and it's all because I lost control of the car that night."

"And you stay in Thora to what? Atone for a car accident that wasn't your fault?"

Shelby lifted off him to glare at him. "You don't get it. I was driving."

"In bad weather that made the roads slippery."

She scooted away from him. "But I should have been more careful."

"You might have been the most cautious driver in the world, but you can't control everything from that night." He reached for her hands. "Shelby, you can't let one moment determine the rest of your life."

"Why not? You're expecting me to let what happened Saturday night decide what happens with us." She shook off his embrace. "You don't know what it's like to be responsible for your family. To stick around and help them out because it's the right thing to do. No, you ran off instead of working things out with your parents." She rose to her feet and started to dust off the sand sticking to the back of her shorts.

"Because that was the right thing for me to do at the time. I had to go, in order to find my own happiness." He stood and held out his arms. "Given the choice again, I'd go again too."

"That's where we disagree, because I can't leave. And I can't push my family aside to pursue my own selfish wishes."

"Wanting what makes you happy doesn't make you selfish."

He stared at her, wishing they didn't have to end their afternoon this way. He wanted to kiss her. To revel in how good it felt for her to be in his arms for those few minutes. Instead, she held herself away from him. He reached out to touch her cheek, but she backed away. "Good luck in the election. You're going to need it."

A flash of emotions were reflected in her eyes. He thought he could see regret, longing, even triumph. Then she was gone.

SHELBY FOUND GREAT-AUNT SARAH in the games room of the seniors' complex playing cards with three other residents. "Well, if it isn't our future mayor." Aunt Sarah pointed to an empty chair nearby. "Pull up a seat and join us."

"I don't want to interrupt you."

The woman across from Aunt Sarah

shook her head and laid down her cards. "Doesn't matter. I'm out. She's bleeding me dry."

Shelby surveyed the table, noticing the coins in the middle of the table. "Are you playing poker?"

Aunt Sarah leaned in and whispered loudly, "I've been on a winning streak this afternoon. I just got a royal flush."

The other players groaned and laid down their cards. Aunt Sarah cackled and pulled the money toward her. When she was done, she glanced at Shelby. "Uh-oh. What happened? You've got that look."

Shelby suddenly clammed up and watched her great-aunt organize the coins by type into small stacks. "Doesn't matter."

"Is it about you kissing a certain mayoral candidate?"

One of the ladies leaned in closer. "Is Josh a good kisser?"

"Gladys, please. The girl's upset." Aunt Sarah turned to her. "But is he? He's got that full bottom lip that I like on a man. And from what I hear, he's had plenty of practice."

"I don't want to talk about it."

"So why are you here, then? Besides interrupting my winning streak?"

Shelby glanced at the trio of ladies, who watched her at first but then started to make excuses and leave the table when they realized that they weren't going to get any juicy details out of her. Shelby picked up the cards they'd left behind and shuffled them to keep her hands busy. "Want to play gin?"

"Now I really know you're upset." Aunt Sarah placed a hand over hers. "A card game isn't going to change anything."

How many times had Shelby run to her nana or great-aunt Sarah for advice? In some ways, she was closer to them than she'd been to her own mother, who loved to tell her what she ought to do in a perfect world. Her great-aunt and grandmother had instead talked more of reality.

Shelby put the cards in their box and handed it to Aunt Sarah. "I just left Josh."

"So that's the reason for the melancholy face."

"I guess."

"You guess or you know?"

"The kiss meant more to me than a photo op on the front page of the local paper."

"And what did it mean to Josh?"

"We decided that we couldn't let it happen again. That the election was more important right now."

"More important than love?"

Shelby pointed to herself. "Did I say love? No, it's more of an infatuation leftover from high school."

"Is that all it is?" Aunt Sarah sounded skeptical. "Then, why are you so sad over it ending?"

Shelby looked up at her. "Because I've discovered that I like the man that he is now more than the boy I once knew." She buried her head into her hands. "Why did it have to happen now of all times? When we're running against each other?"

"In my experience, love doesn't often choose a convenient time to appear." She sighed and leaned back in her chair. "I've told you about Henry."

Shelby sighed and wondered if she'd be sitting at a table in a seniors' home telling Harper about Josh one day.

"This is the end of your love story with Josh, then?"

"Has to be, don't you think? Only one

of us can win the election. We're both so passionate about being mayor, I'm not sure the one who loses will be able to get past it. Maybe that disappointment would always be between us." Shelby took a deep breath and offered one sharp nod. "It is over."

"There's more to my story with Henry that I haven't told you. That he's still living. In this very seniors' home, in fact." Shelby stared at her, but Aunt Sarah refused to meet her eyes as she continued, "I knew he was in town after he left me. Knew he got married to someone else. Had kids. Then got divorced. Got married again. A few years ago, after she died, he reached out to me. To ask for forgiveness, he claimed. But I wouldn't listen to him. I let the bitterness that I'd held on to so tightly keep us apart, even now."

"So you know what I mean."

"I know that misread feelings can't replace what might have been. If I had looked beyond my pride instead and given Henry another chance…" She reached out to Shelby, holding her hand palm up until Shelby put her own on top. "I could have had my moment with Henry. And I still could now if I'd only take that chance, but I'm afraid of getting hurt, just like you are with Josh. I don't want you to miss out on a happier ending."

CHAPTER SEVEN

JOSH CHECKED HIS watch to find that he still had a couple of minutes before the press conference started. He couldn't wait to make the announcement that would boost his campaign's chances of winning. Cosart stood next to him, surveying the paltry showing but didn't criticize. They'd hammered out the details of the deal until the wee hours of the morning in anticipation of this statement. While Cosart wanted to keep the focus on the factory and the business, Josh knew they had to emphasize the jobs that the factory would bring. Good-paying jobs with benefits would attract workers to the town.

Josh froze when he saw Shelby standing next to her father. It had been almost a week since they'd argued and said goodbye. Why did she have to look so beautiful in a blue blouse that matched her eyes? She looked back at him, unblinking.

He turned away from her. *Focus on the campaign, Riley. This is about jobs. And about boosting the economy. And becoming mayor. Don't be intimidated by a pair of sparkling blue eyes.*

Tim touched Josh's elbow and leaned into him. "It's time. Don't forget to make sure to point out that it was your idea to bring Cosart here. That it was your proposal that won him over."

"I've rehearsed this speech a million times. I've got this."

"You better."

Josh approached the rail bordering the ramp that led inside the shipping department of the old Russell Tire factory. Cosart stayed a few steps behind as he'd agreed to do until Josh introduced him. "Thank you all for coming out to this monumental announcement for Thora and its citizens. As you all know, I have been working hard to bring Cosart Industries to town to discuss how we can form a beneficial relationship. One that will profit all of us. And I'm pleased to announce that Mr. Cosart will be hiring upward of ten thousand people here this fall when he expands his business to include this very factory."

A smattering of applause followed. "I know that my opponent is not in favor of this move." He sought out Shelby in the audience. "She believes that we can't depend on an outside company to swoop in and rescue us. But I would say to her, we don't need to be rescued. What we do need is to roll up our sleeves and work together with corporations and thus save ourselves."

Josh smiled at Cosart. "Without further ado, Larry Cosart."

Josh stepped back as the CEO spoke of his plan to expand his company to the Midwest by starting with Thora. To bring manufacturing back to a town that had seen too many of its factories shuttered and laid empty. Josh let his mind wander. He'd done his job and brought in business. Even if he wasn't elected mayor, this move would benefit the town. He just hoped this would bring the boost his campaign needed.

When Cosart finished, Josh spoke up again. "I hope that this is the beginning of a boom for Thora. A beginning that, as mayor,

I will expand upon until we all achieve a better tomorrow with higher-paying jobs, better STEM programs for schools and a wider tax base to fund our town's public safety officers and city services."

Tim joined him and Cosart. "Thank you, Josh. Do we have any questions?"

Drew from the Thora Press raised his hand. "Josh, is it true that you and your opponent are now dating?"

Josh sighed. He supposed the question was inevitable, especially from Drew, given it had been his article with the kissing photo that had been published. Again, he searched out Shelby in the audience. "No. What your camera caught was just a moment between two people. That's all it was. A moment. And trust me, it won't happen again."

Shelby blinked at him, then slipped away, her father trailing behind her.

"So the rumors that you are putting your support behind her campaign—"

"Are unfounded and completely ridiculous. I'm still running for mayor and intend to win. Next question?"

Once he and Cosart had answered all of the questions, Josh thanked everyone for coming. Thinking he was alone, he tugged off his tie and shoved it into his pocket. Feeling a hand on his shoulder, he turned to find Melanie standing there. "Congratulations on Cosart. This should give you a surge in the polls."

He looked around. "Is Shelby with you?"

"She went back to the garage with her dad. Why?"

He gave a shrug as if it didn't matter. "You didn't come here just to congratulate me. What do you want, Mel?"

"Stay away from Shelby."

"Is this coming from you or her?"

"Don't distract her from the campaign." Melanie took a step toward him. "She's worked hard to get where she is, and she doesn't deserve to have something or someone come between her and what she wants."

"How do you know what she really wants?"

Melanie put her hands on her hips. "I'm her best friend, who she tells everything to. Trust me. I know what she wants."

"Are you sure about that? Because as I see it, she's kept secrets from you and her family."

"And you think that she's confided them

to you?" Melanie chuckled. "Give me a break. Shelby had a moment of weakness last Saturday night, but I assure you that it's over. And you don't know anything about her, so don't delude yourself that you do."

Melanie stomped away while Josh wondered if maybe she was right. What did he really know about Shelby anyway? And why did he want to get closer to her, given the obstacles in front of them?

Maybe because those obstacles were trivial. Considering the big picture, things like the election result and possible trouble in her family weren't deal breakers, compared to what other people had to overcome.

Josh ran a hand over his face. When had he become so besotted with Shelby Cuthbert? He needed something to get her out of his system.

Or maybe someone else.

Wondering if Alyssa might still be interested in a date, he got out his tie and tried to convince himself that one pair of bright blue eyes didn't matter.

And that Shelby would be better off without him.

PENNY'S WEDDING PLANNING had been going really well, but she'd hit a snag and had called Shelby for an emergency meeting with Aunt Sarah at the seniors' home. Despite the demands of her campaign, Shelby made the time to meet them and to bring dinner with her.

Shelby nudged the box of pizza closer to Aunt Sarah. "There's one piece left with your name on it."

Aunt Sarah glanced it at, but shook her head. "If anyone's name is on it, it's Penny."

"Mine? I have a wedding dress that I'm going to need to fit into next month. The pizza belongs to Shelby."

Shelby grinned and snagged the slice of pizza from the box. "Fine. It's all mine."

Penny pulled the notebook around to her side of the table to look over Shelby's notes on the guest list. "I should have asked you to help me from the beginning."

"Why didn't you?"

"Because you were involved with the campaign, and I figured that it wouldn't be that difficult to plan a simple wedding." She winced. "As you can see, the plan for simple went out the window a while ago. Who knew that Christopher and I had so many friends and family?"

"Well, the family is mostly on your side," Aunt Sarah said. "The Cuthberts seem to grow exponentially every year."

"True. But with Christopher's position here at the home, and my job at the fire department, we've made a lot of friends in the community. And now with the caterer dropping out, I'm scrambling to figure out what we're going to feed all these guests."

"Have you checked with Aunt June about a caterer?"

"This was her recommendation. But Lana is going to be in Colorado caring for her mother for the foreseeable future." Penny sighed and swiped her hair off her face. "I've been calling everyone I know for ideas, but all the good caterers are already booked for that weekend."

Shelby looked over at Aunt Sarah. "What about the caterer we use for the Christmas fundraiser? He's reasonably priced."

"He's one of the caterers who already has a job that weekend," Aunt Sarah answered. "Penny's right. Everyone seems to have been booked."

Shelby leaned back in the chair. "We're going to have to look outside the box, meaning not at the usual caterers from the sounds of it."

A knock on the door interrupted their brainstorming. Aunt Sarah rose slowly and walked across the room to answer it. Mr. Duffy was in his wheelchair on the other side of the door. "I didn't realize you had company, Sarah. I'll come back another time."

He wheeled his chair away as Aunt Sarah stood staring after him. When she eventually closed the door and returned to the sofa, her cheeks were pink. Penny peered at her. "Why was Mr. Duffy knocking on your door?"

Aunt Sarah shook her head. "I have no idea. Now, how about we get back to Shelby's notion about looking outside of our usual caterers."

Shelby held up a hand to pause the proceedings. "I'm more interested in hearing why he was seeking you out. What does he want to talk to you about?"

"It's nothing."

But the telltale blush on her cheeks that

now extended down her neck and chest seemed to contradict her words. Shelby leaned forward. "Are you interested in Mr. Duffy? Romantically?"

Aunt Sarah pointed at the two of them. "What I am is none of your business, romantically or otherwise. We're here to discuss Penny's important wedding plans, and that's what we're going to do."

Shelby and Penny exchanged a look, but let the matter drop. "Fine, Aunt Sarah. You can keep your secrets." Shelby switched back to Penny. "Do you and Christopher have a favorite restaurant that might be interested in providing the food at the hall? Or I've even heard of couples hiring food trucks instead of a typical caterer. That might be a possibility."

The rest of the conversation centered on the wedding, although Shelby kept wondering what Mr. Duffy had been planning to tell her great-aunt.

SHELBY READ THE article detailing Josh's announcement and slammed the local Sunday paper on her parents' kitchen table. It was reported that several citizens seemed to think that the arrival of the factory would result in a surge to Josh's polling numbers. According to Melanie, Josh still had a ways to go before he could beat her. Shelby wanted to feel confident, but instead, she was concerned.

Caffeine would help, she thought, and she refilled her mug. Leaning on the counter, she looked at her father, who had picked up the newspaper to read the article. "Is it petty of me to resent this factory that will bring in jobs for the town? Shouldn't I be happy that we can put more of our people back to work?" she asked.

"I think you resent the fact that it's Josh who is responsible for the factory reopening." He held out his mug, and she used the carafe to refill it. "You've still got this election in the bag, honey. Don't you worry about that."

"That's the thing, Dad. I am worried." She returned to the table to sit across from him. "What if I lose?"

"Not going to happen."

"But it could. I've been putting in the time and effort for this, but it could all be for nothing." She took a deep breath and released it, hooking one arm over the back of her chair. "What I need is something bigger than Cosart to help Thora. The problem is that I'm out of ideas."

"What if you build on what Josh has already done? Use the factory coming here to bring about other programs that you've been wanting to implement. If Cosart Industries brings us the expected surge of jobs and families to the community, then what could you do to piggyback on that to benefit the town? This isn't an either-or situation, sweetie. This is a win-win for Thora."

Shelby gave a nod. "I know you're right. I just hate to see Josh's campaign surge in the polls. I'm still ahead, but the gap is narrowing."

Her mother entered the kitchen, wearing her striped bathrobe and slippers, and planted a kiss on her father's forehead before placing a hand on Shelby's shoulder. "You're here early for a Sunday morning."

Shelby pointed to the bakery box on the counter. "Couldn't sleep, so I stopped and got pastries to share."

Her mother grabbed a cinnamon roll and had a large bite before taking the seat next to her father, who handed her the Thora paper. "So I see Josh got more press."

"At least we weren't kissing on the front page this time."

Her mother made a face. "I hope that was the last time that happens." She peered at Shelby. "That was the only time, wasn't it?" Shelby didn't answer, and her mother huffed. "Really? I don't understand this fascination that you have with him."

"It's leftovers from a schoolgirl crush. It's nothing," Shelby reassured.

"It better be nothing because he's trouble with a capital *T*."

"That's in his past. You don't know the man that he's become now."

"And you do?"

Shelby flattened her crumpled napkin on the table, smoothing it out. "Better than most in this town, yes." She lifted her eyes to look at her mom. "He's a good man."

"Because he brought a factory to town?"

"Because he came back to Thora to take care of Bert. Josh cleans and cooks for him. Takes him to the doctor and makes sure he's taking his medication. All of this for a man who hasn't made it a secret how much his son has disappointed him. And he's doing more than giving lip service to what he wants to do for Thora. He's trying to implement a mentoring program for at-risk kids in the schools, like he did in Pittsburgh. I admire him for that."

Her father cleared his throat. "Admire him all you want, Shelby, but don't let it come between you and this election. You're the one who deserves to be mayor."

"I'm not so sure about that anymore." The shocked silence made Shelby shake her head. "Forget I said that. It's just my nerves talking."

"Only sixteen days until the election. What have you got planned this week?" Dad asked.

"Speech at the seniors' center. A fundraiser for the fire department. And I hope to do some more door-to-door campaigning."

"Anything you need from us, just say the word." Her mom smiled.

Shelby smiled at her parents. "If only your confidence in me could win the election."

But Shelby couldn't shake this feeling that she was losing ground in the race to be mayor. If she wasn't careful, it would be too late to get her momentum back and win.

LATER THAT DAY, she pondered how to gain more votes as she waited for her carryout from her favorite Mexican restaurant. She sat in the lobby and typed a fresh thought into her phone, pausing when she heard a familiar voice. Standing to peek around the corner, she checked out the dining room and spotted Josh sitting in a booth, sharing a bowl of chips and salsa with Alyssa Winfield. Her eyes widened as her heart seemed to drop into her stomach.

When had he started seeing Alyssa? He obviously hadn't waited long after kissing her. She turned back to hide out in the lobby. The sooner her California burrito dinner was ready, the better. She opened her phone but couldn't see the keys or form a thought in her head.

"Shelby." She looked up to see Josh staring down at her. "I thought that was you."

Shelby tried to smile but realized it probably was more like a grimace. "I'm just waiting for my food."

"Cuthbert," the hostess called and held up a carryout container. "You're all set, sweetie."

Shelby almost leaped forward and accepted her dinner. "Nice to see you again, Josh. Enjoy the rest of your evening with Alyssa."

She quickly exited the restaurant, but Josh was too fast for her and caught up. "Shelby, wait. It's not what you think."

"It doesn't matter what I think. You're a grown man who can see anyone you want." She kept walking, though her pace had definitely slowed. She needed to work out more.

"But I don't want Alyssa. Not like I want…"

He stopped talking and walking, but she knew he'd been about to say *you*. The unspoken word seemed to hang in the air between them. She told herself to get moving, yet her feet ignored her.

"Have a good night, Shelby. I'm sure I'll be seeing you soon."

She watched him return to the restaurant. He glanced back at her when he reached the door, then turned to go inside, shaking his head.

JOSH LEANED DOWN and placed the bouquet of daisies next to the headstone before resting a hand on it. He ran a finger over the imprinted letters of his mother's name, Barbara Ann Riley. "Happy birthday, Mom. I miss you so much."

He swallowed at the regret that rested at the back of his throat. It was his own fault that he'd missed out on spending her birthdays with her when she'd been alive. If he had dealt with his pride and showed up instead of sending a gift and making a phone call, then he might not be missing her so much now. Covering his eyes, he rubbed a hand over his forehead.

"Didn't think I'd see you here today."

He turned at the sound of his father's voice and saw the old man standing behind him, a daisy bouquet in his hands. "Why wouldn't I want to visit her today?"

His dad brushed past him and laid his bouquet next to his own. "A little too late, if you ask me."

"I know, Dad. You don't have to tell me that. I have enough regrets."

His dad looked at Josh's bouquet. "You remembered that she loved daisies."

His mom had always said that roses were

pretentious, but daisies provided just as much beauty for being a simple flower.

The two men stood looking at the grave marker, silent in their thoughts. Josh swallowed again and wondered how long it would take for him to release this guilt. Too many years he'd stayed away. Too many holidays he'd spent alone in Pittsburgh, rather than risk being rejected by his parents.

He closed his eyes again, squatted to put his hand on the grass over his mother's grave. A tear fell slowly down his cheek, and Josh took a deep gulp of air.

He felt his father put a hand on his shoulder. "She really missed you."

Josh straightened to stare down at the grave. "I really missed her too."

"Then why didn't you come back sooner?"

Josh shook his head. "It doesn't matter anymore."

"No doubt she would have gotten a kick out of seeing you run for mayor."

"But she wouldn't have voted for me, right?"

"Don't say that. She was better at seeing how you'd changed."

"I haven't really changed all that much."

"I don't know about that. I've been listening to what you're saying in terms of what the town needs. I've seen how you've taken action to help the town, regardless of the election. I think you might be the right man for mayor, after all."

Josh stared at his father. "Are you saying you'd vote for me?"

"I guess I am. I really like Shelby, don't get me wrong. And yes, she'd make an amazing mayor. But I believe you've changed my mind."

Josh didn't say anything, afraid that if he did that, he'd mess up this moment. His dad hadn't said that he was proud of him or anything. Or that he'd been forgiven. But earning his dad's vote felt like a step in the right direction.

JOSH APPRECIATED THE warm greeting from the senior citizens who had gathered to hear the candidates' speeches. One woman stopped him, holding on to his forearm. "Why, Joshua Riley, you've grown into a strapping young man. The pictures in the paper don't do you justice."

He patted her hand on his. "Thank you, ma'am."

"Call me Sarah."

"Well, thank you, Sarah." He hooked a thumb toward the podium. "I should get over there. They're expecting me."

"They'll wait for you. I want to chat with you for a second."

Josh let his hand drop and stood before the woman who looked to be in her mid-eighties. "I'm always happy to talk to a concerned citizen."

"I'm also Shelby's great-aunt."

He glanced around the room to see if Shelby had set him up. "I see."

"Don't worry. She doesn't know I'm waylaying you." She patted the metal folding chair next to her. "Why don't you take a seat?"

Curious about what Sarah had to tell him, he dropped onto the chair and folded his legs at his ankles. "What's on your mind, Sarah?"

"What are your intentions?"

Josh felt his heart stop for a moment. "Do you mean for Thora?"

The woman smiled at him as if he'd made

a good joke. "What else could I have meant? Unless, well, for my niece?"

He was afraid that had been what she'd meant. Hoping to avoid answering, he tried to stick to the election instead. "I plan on helping rebuild Thora's workforce by bringing businesses into the community as well as emphasizing science and technology in our school's curriculum so that our children will be set up for success in the future."

"You sound like you have a solid plan for the town's future."

"I certainly hope so. I've been hammering home those points over the last month."

"And what of your own future?"

She peered at him closely, and he stammered. "Uh. T-to work hard to benefit Thora, of course. That's my focus right now."

She looked disappointed at his response. "You're not married. Do you plan to be?"

"I don't know see how that is relevant to my campaign."

She took a deep breath. "Let me get to the point, Josh. My niece Shelby is an amazing woman who doesn't come along every day. While there may be others out there, and we both know who I'm talking about…" She paused to elbow him. "Don't be rash. You'd be a fool to let Shelby slip from your fingers."

His mouth opened and shut several times before he got to his feet. "I'll take that under advisement, Sarah."

"You'd best move fast, young man, before she gets swept up by someone else with more courage than you."

SHELBY CLUTCHED HER note cards and noticed Mr. Duffy wheeling his chair closer to her. "Ms. Cuthbert, I expect to hear great things from you today."

She remembered him from the previous times she'd visited the center, before Aunt Sarah had moved in. "Thank you, Mr. Duffy. I believe you will."

"Call me Henry."

Shelby stopped and stared at him. "As in Aunt Sarah's Henry?" He looked around the room before giving a soft nod. Surprised, she tried to imagine him as a younger man. "She told me that you lived here."

"So she's spoken of me."

"My cousins and I have all heard the story of how you left her at the altar."

"I was a fool. I have no excuse, and then it always seemed too late."

Mr. Duffy pointed to an empty chair not too far away. "Would you mind sitting down? It's hard to talk with you standing over me."

"Of course." She knew she should practice her speech but took the seat and focused on him. Her curiosity was piqued. "Is there something you want to tell me?"

His jaw seemed to be chewing over his words before he spoke. "I made a mistake, one that I've always regretted. And I want a second chance."

"So why are you speaking to me?"

"Because your aunt respects your opinion. And this old man thought maybe if I could win you over to my side, you might plead my case with her." He took one of her hands in his wrinkled one. "I truly loved her, but I let my own pride get in the way and lost her. If I could go back, I would choose a life with her above everything else. And I may not have long left on this earth, but I'd rather spend every single minute I have with her by my side."

His eyes misted with tears, and Shelby felt her heart soften toward him. She squeezed his hand. "Henry, if anyone is to plead your case with Aunt Sarah, it should be you. She'll respect you more for it."

"I finally got up enough nerve to show up at her door last week, but—"

"Penny and I were there, so you couldn't talk then."

He nodded. "And I don't really know what I'd say, if I got up the courage to try again."

"You did a pretty good job admitting to me how you felt about her." She looked over her shoulder to where her aunt sat talking with Josh. Now, what was that about? She turned back to Henry. "Just talk to her. I think she's ready to listen."

She gave him a smile, hoping to encourage him, then joined Christopher waiting at the podium. "I see Mr. Duffy waylaid you. I hope he didn't complain too much."

She looked back at Henry and then at her aunt, who waved at her. "Actually, he wanted to talk about something else that completely surprised me." She gave Christopher a smile. "And he gave me a lot to think about."

Christopher gave her an odd look, then welcomed Josh, as well. Shelby gave Josh a nod. Had he thought about her as much as she had of him? Did he regret their fight and how things had ended? Did he dream of her?

Josh held his hand out to her, and she shook it, letting the grip on him linger for longer than was necessary. She peered into his eyes and let go, taking a step away. "Congratulations on Cosart. That's a humongous feather in your cap."

His gaze stayed on hers as he said softly, "But you're still ahead in the polls."

"You're gaining on me. That's something, at least."

"Shelby, about Alyssa…"

Whatever he meant to say was interrupted by Christopher introducing both candidates to the seniors gathered. They took their positions on either side of the director. By earlier agreement, Shelby spoke first.

She knew she gave the speech she had prepared, though she couldn't recall the specifics of what she was saying. Even as she spoke, her mind drifted to Josh, who stood near to her. What had he been about to tell her? Was he suffering as much as she was by this forced distance separating them?

She stepped aside once she finished and focused on Josh's back as he began his speech. She didn't pay attention to the words but to the passion behind them. He really would be good for Thora as mayor. He had solid ideas that would need some finessing of the town council members, but he believed in what he shared with the audience. By the end of his speech, she was almost willing to vote for him herself.

After the speeches, refreshments were brought out, and both candidates circulated around the room. Even as she spoke to different seniors about their concerns for Thora, she was aware of Josh's location every moment. She could hear his laugh when he joked with a group of women. And found herself smiling along with it.

"He was good up there," Aunt Sarah said as she approached with a cup of tea and a plate of cookies. "Of course, he wasn't as good as you were. I bet you gained a bunch of votes today."

"You'll never guess who I talked to earlier." When Aunt Sarah watched her without guessing, Shelby continued, "Your Henry."

"He's hardly mine anymore."

"You said he wants to be though. Have you thought about it?"

"And what of your Josh? Have you thought about that?"

"Those are two different things, Aunt Sarah, and you know it."

"What I understand is that we're both afraid to let them get too close to us."

Shelby shook her head. "I'm not scared of Josh."

"What if he hurts you again? And you're left on the porch, crying your eyes out, wondering what you did that was so wrong for him to leave you?"

"You might be fearful of letting Henry into your life again, but I don't have a choice. I can't pursue anything with Josh. At least, not right now."

"And what if when the timing is perfect in your mind, it's already too late? You work so hard to control everything in your world, but this isn't something where you can dictate when it's allowed to happen. Give him a chance."

Shelby stared at her aunt for a long moment before she said, "He doesn't want me, so there's nothing to give."

"No, what you're really afraid of is that he does want you."

IT WAS BUZZING at Melanie's bookstore, especially at the coffee bar, so Shelby took a seat in the romance section and plucked one of the Regency books off the shelf to read while she waited. She'd made it to chapter three, where the duke dressed down Lady Whistler, when Mel took the armchair next to hers. "Thanks for coming by. How was the speech?"

Shelby put one finger in the book to keep her place. "The seniors love me. Most of them remember me as the woman who brings home-baked cookies every month and organizes game nights to raise money for the community garden."

"I never doubted we had the senior citizen vote." Melanie peered at her. "How did Josh do?"

"The Cosart deal will help him, but probably not with the seniors. Though rumor has it that the mayor is about to endorse him. That will win them over to his side."

"You don't know for sure that Bill is going to put his weight behind Josh. I heard that he refuses to endorse either one of you because he wants to remain impartial." Melanie gave a shrug. "Though an endorsement from him could backfire depending on how the voters view his affair."

"We have fourteen days left. I need more than just the mayor's approval or otherwise. I need something that will slow down Josh's rise in the polls. Any ideas?"

"Several, but are you willing to listen to them?"

"I always listen. I just don't always agree with them." Shelby grinned at her friend and nudged her with her shoulder. "By the way, I'm not going to be able to make it to the movie tonight with you and Jack. I've got too much to do with the election, and I have to catch up on some things at the garage."

Melanie peered at her. "That's weak,

Shelby. Why don't you just say that you don't want to go with us?"

"Maybe I'm trying to give you two a night alone. Have you told him anything about your feelings?" Melanie bit her lip and glanced away. Shelby reached over to take her friend's hand. "What will it hurt to finally let him know that you're in love with him?"

"I could lose the best friend I ever had." Mel glanced at her. "Except for you, of course." She smiled weakly and looked down at her lap. "If I keep my feelings to myself, then at least I still have Jack in my life."

"But you're not happy."

"Happiness is overrated sometimes."

"What if he's waiting for you to make the first move? What if he's just as afraid as you are to take things to the next level?"

"And what if he doesn't have these feelings for me? At least if I don't say anything, that possibility of us as a couple still exists. Even if it's only in my mind." She shook her head. "But if I tell him and he doesn't reciprocate, I could lose everything."

Shelby rubbed Mel's shoulder. "He'd be

an idiot to let you get away. And we both know he's not an idiot."

Melanie stood. "I've got to get back to work. And you're going to the movie tonight. No arguments. I'm not ready to tell Jack." She started to take a step away, muttering, "I don't know if I ever will be."

THE JUBILANT MOOD at the sports bar after the local college football team's victory over its major rival made it difficult for Josh to hear what Tim was saying. He leaned closer. "Did you say that the poll numbers haven't changed since the Cosart announcement?"

"No, what I said is that we need another surge like Cosart to put you over the top. Otherwise, you're looking at conceding to Shelby on Election Day."

Josh toyed with a french fry and then threw it down on his plate. "I'm out of ideas. I keep hammering on the key points of my platform. Jobs. Education. Better city services. What more do the voters want from me?"

Tim rubbed a finger over his upper lip. "I have something, but I'm not sure you're going to like it." He picked up a folder from the seat next to him and slid it across the table to Josh. "We've avoided attacks on character, but this might be the right time to bring this out."

Josh pushed the file back across the table. "I told you at the beginning, no personal attacks. And I'm not changing my mind about that."

"It's not an attack on Shelby. Besides, how badly do you want to win?"

He thought of his father and the wide gulf that still seemed to separate them. Josh put his hand on the folder. "Before I look at this, we have to agree that it's my choice whether we use this information or not."

"Just open it."

Josh flipped aside the cover of the folder and skimmed the police report inside. Then flipped that over to read the affidavit that followed. He lifted his eyes to Tim. "You're sure this information is accurate?"

"My partner was the police officer on scene. He wouldn't lie to me."

Josh read through it a second time, then closed the file and slid it across to Tim. The information here would hurt Shelby's chances because it would bring damage to the Cuthberts and how folks regarded them. Her family meant everything to her. Even more than the town did. On the other hand, it would help his campaign, but at what cost? "I need to think about this."

"Well, don't think too long. We need to be in Sunday's paper if we're going to use it in time to make a difference." Tim tossed the folder to Josh's side of the booth. "I know you'll do the right thing."

CHAPTER EIGHT

THE BOLT WOULDN'T tighten like it should, and Shelby wondered if it should be replaced. It could be stripped. But that would prevent it from sitting tight and might cause leaks in the radiator. Or worse.

"So this is where you hide yourself nine to five."

Shelby bumped her head on the chassis and muffled a curse. She spotted a pair of worn tennis shoes beside the car. Using the chassis for leverage, she scooted the cart to the opposite side of the vehicle, then took her time getting up. A nearby rag helped her wipe off most of the grease from her hands. "Your car giving you problems, Josh?"

He looked across the hood at her, shaking his head. "I was wondering if you had time for a little chat."

"Little chat? No. Business has been picking up, and I'm swamped."

He glanced around the near-empty garage and cocked his head to one side.

"Fine. My office is in the back. I'll meet you inside once I wash my hands off."

"Actually, this is something better discussed in private."

"My office does have a door that closes."

"More private than that. How about a drive up to the lake tonight when you get out of work? That way, I don't take you away from your busy schedule."

"I don't think that's a good idea. I thought we agreed not to be seen together?"

"This is completely innocent, Shelby." He lifted his chin. "Or are you afraid of being alone with me?"

"Fine. But I'm driving. Be here no later than four thirty."

Josh gave her a smile that made her belly flutter. He winked. "See you then."

INSIDE CAMPAIGN HEADQUARTERS set up in the garage, Tim drummed his fingers on the table as Josh read over the invoice for the printer. There had been a recent demand for more yard signs, a good indicator in Tim's opinion. Josh's too. That meant more people had changed their minds about him. And if the poll numbers were close to accurate, he only needed another small push to put him on top.

Josh gave a nod and wrote out a check from the campaign fund account he'd arranged at the local bank. "This is money well spent, I'd say."

"The printer will have the signs ready by Friday. These could mean victory for us." Tim took the check and started to rise from his seat. "By the way, have you thought about using that story on the Cuthberts?"

Josh frowned. He'd thought about little else. In fact, that's why he'd made a date to meet up with Shelby that evening. He wanted to give her a chance to respond to these allegations before he did anything. "I haven't decided what I want to do yet."

"Time is growing shorter, so think faster." Tim pointed absently to the street beyond the open garage. "I know that the people who live here think they are all great and everything, but the Cuthbert family are not who they seem. And that's what that file proves."

"Why do you hate the Cuthberts so much?" It was the one thing that Josh kept coming back to. Revealing this story seemed to be personal for Tim, rather than for some sense of civic duty.

Tim scowled. "Because I've given my life to the police force and Chief Cuthbert denied my promotion not once, but twice."

"So, this is personal—"

"No. This is politics." Tim rapped his knuckles on the table. "Let's use the story and win this election already."

Josh still wasn't convinced. "I'm not sure that's the best option."

"Then maybe you don't want to do what it takes to win."

"I want to win the right way."

Tim rolled his eyes and left the garage, almost bumping into Josh's dad. Josh checked the time. "Sorry, that went longer than I expected it to. I'll make our lunch now."

His dad's eyes followed the direction of Tim's retreat. "What was that all about?"

"Nothing for you to worry about. What are you hungry for?"

"What is he asking you to do?"

"Dad, it's nothing. Okay?"

"I wasn't sure about you asking Tim to

be your campaign manager. Based on what I just overheard, I'm even more skeptical."

Josh couldn't figure out what his father was trying to say. "What's wrong with Tim?"

"I heard that he blames the Cuthberts for not getting his promotion, but he didn't qualify under Chief Winters either." His dad paused as if expecting Josh to agree. "Have you asked yourself why?"

Josh rubbed his jaw, offering an answer. "It's not the person in charge of the department that's the reason, but Tim himself that's kept him from moving up the chain." He nodded, finally catching on. "I've thought that too."

"I'd hate to see you lose because of Tim."

Josh raised his eyebrows at this. "You really think I could win?"

His dad made a gruff noise and waved off the comment. "All I'm saying is, I'd be careful with Tim." He started to turn. "But yeah, you might have a chance."

Josh squelched his grin and followed his dad into the kitchen to prepare their lunch. He was getting closer to winning, and with his dad too.

THE HOURS UNTIL her date with Josh passed so slowly. Too slowly. And besides, it wasn't a date. They were going for a drive and having a chat.

A chat about what? That's the part that made Shelby nervous.

Josh arrived twenty minutes early and spent that time talking with her employees, especially Eddie, who laughed at something he said. Shelby narrowed her eyes. Eddie never laughed at something she said. But then, she'd been accused by an old boyfriend of being dull and decidedly unfunny.

She saved the updated inventory file on her computer, then switched it off before grabbing her purse. When she walked out of the office, Josh whistled at her. "You clean up good, Cuthbert."

Shelby looked down at the plain top and basic blue jeans she wore. "You can stop being charming. It doesn't work on me."

"Is that what I was doing?"

Shelby turned to Eddie. "If you don't mind locking up, I'm leaving a little early tonight."

"You're the boss."

She cocked her head toward the back door. "The Mustang's out this way."

"We're taking that old thing? Are you sure it's safe?"

"Relax. It's been fixed." She opened the door and waited for him to pass through first before joining him outside. The wall of heat hit her like a slap in the face. "It's been a scorcher this summer."

"Actually, it's the humidity that's up. Makes it feel worse."

She shot him a look. "Hot is hot, no matter the humidity."

They had reached the Mustang, and she slid into the driver's seat while Josh waited on the other side. She reached over the length of the seat to pop up the lock. "You've got to love these old cars," Josh said as he ran a hand along the leather interior. "None of the modern conveniences, but they definitely have style."

Shelby started the car, and they pulled out onto the street, catching the curious looks of pedestrians on the sidewalk. "I bet our being seen together is about to be telegraphed on the Thora gossip express."

Josh smiled and put an arm along the

back of her bucket seat so that his fingers dangled above her shoulder. "Let them talk. We're just going for a ride."

Shelby headed toward the highway that would take them to the lakeshore. "You also said we're chatting. So do it, already."

Josh rolled the window down with the hand crank. "It can wait. I'm enjoying the feel of fresh air on my face." He closed his eyes and let out a deep sigh. "That's what I'm talking about."

She put on the radio, which had been tuned to a classic rock station. A classic car deserved music just as classic. They drove for almost an hour with the radio their only soundtrack until Shelby reached a small lakefront town and parked the Mustang off the main street. It was a nice change being able to be comfortable with their silence. She turned to Josh. "Had enough fresh air?"

He looked over at her. "Not nearly enough. Let's walk while we talk."

They took their time window shopping along the avenue of stores until they reached the lighthouse on the St. Clair River. Pausing on the shoreline, they stood watching a big ship pass. "It's a beautiful night, don't you think?" Josh asked as he surveyed the horizon. "Blue skies with wisps of clouds. Ships sailing. And I'm looking across the river to Canada."

Shelby shielded her eyes with one hand as she turned to look at him. "Did you bring me out here to spout poetry?"

He pointed to a bench that waited a dozen yards away. "Why don't we take a seat?"

Once settled, she waited for Josh to share what was on his mind, but he didn't expand on his thoughts. Instead, he kept his gaze on the river. She wondered what he was thinking about as he watched the ships. She always wondered where these ships had come from and where they were headed to. What would her life be like if she could jump on one of them and sail off to somewhere far away?

"I got some information the other day that has me troubled."

Shelby put a hand on his arm. "Is it your dad? Is he okay?"

He turned to look at her and smiled into her eyes. "He's fine, but this isn't about my family, Shelby. It's about yours. And it's not good news." He pulled two sheets of paper from his jeans pocket and handed them to her. "You might want to read these."

She felt her spine straighten and her belly tighten at his words. Her fingers trembling, she unfolded the pages and read through the first one quickly. Closed her eyes, then read it again before turning to the second. "Who else knows about this?"

"Tim brought it to my attention. He served at the time with the arresting officer."

Shelby let out a breath that she didn't know she'd been holding. The fact that Laurel had been charged with a suspected driving under the influence offence was not a huge surprise. Laurel had been struggling at the time with alcohol, but Harper's birth had turned her life around for the better. It was the actions of her uncle who had been Thora's chief of police at the time of the arrest that shocked her. "And you believe the officer's word?"

"I don't have any reason not to."

She shot off the bench and walked to the river's edge. Josh followed her. "What is this, then? Last-minute blackmail to get me to quit the race?"

"What? No."

"So why bring me out here and drop this bomb into my lap?"

"I'm not going to put out that information. You have to believe me."

"Why not? You want to win, don't you?"

He put his hands on her upper arms. "Yes, I do. But not like that."

She pushed away from him and stared out at the water. "My uncle Bob is one of the most honorable men I know. Niece or not, he wouldn't pressure the officer to scratch the charges against Laurel." She looked up at Josh. "This is some kind of mistake. It has to be."

Josh held up his hands. "Maybe it's all a misunderstanding. Talk to your uncle. See what he says. If he's as honorable as you claim, then you don't have to worry." He gently rubbed her shoulder. "I thought you should know about this because if Tim discovered it, other people could too. But they won't hear about it from me. You've got my word."

She raised her eyes to meet his. And she believed him.

JOSH PUT HIS hand on the back of Shelby's neck as they drove back to Thora. He pointed at a restaurant. "We could stop at the Fish Company for dinner. It's Wednesday, so it's all-you-can-eat shrimp night."

"I'm not hungry."

"Who would be, after the information I gave you?" Although, the restaurant's smoked salmon dip with crostini sounded amazing at the moment. He made a note to come back, perhaps with Shelby once the election was over. "You know, I wish we could both win this election. Maybe share the position of mayor. I'll take a month, and you take the next."

"That's not how it works."

"But wouldn't it be nice? Then we wouldn't be at war." Shelby took her eyes off the road to look at him, and he let his finger run up her bare neck. "And we could kiss whenever we wanted to."

"I thought we agreed not to let it happen again."

"Can't blame a man for wishing."

She rested her gaze back on the car in front of them. "Well, it's not going to happen. Besides, wouldn't Alyssa have a problem with you kissing me?"

"We went out once for dinner, but we both agreed to remain friends."

Shelby snorted. "Friends like we're friends?"

"Is that what we are?"

She gave a one shoulder shrug. "I guess we are, such as it is."

"Why haven't you ever married?"

She stopped at a red light and turned again to look at him. "Why do you want to know?"

"Because it would reveal where the heads of the men in Thora are at."

She gave a shrug. "Guess they don't like what they see."

"From where I'm sitting, there's plenty of good to look at. That auburn hair that curls at the end. Those big blue eyes. Even the freckles on your nose. It makes an attractive package."

Shelby brought up a hand to cover her nose. "Maybe they don't like how bossy I am. I've been accused of being controlling."

"So, there have been men."

A car horn behind them reminded Shelby that the light had turned green. She pressed down on the accelerator and sped through the intersection. "A couple. But they're no business of yours."

"Come on, I thought we just agreed that we're at least friends."

She didn't answer at first, and Josh watched her emotions warring over her face as if debating whether to open that area of her life to him. Finally, she gave a shrug. "I had one serious relationship a few years ago. At least, I thought it was serious and heading toward marriage, but like I told you before, he had other ideas." She gripped the steering wheel a little tighter. "You?"

"Nothing."

She raised an eyebrow at this. "Nothing at all?"

"There have been women, but nothing serious. They tend to get annoyed when I get caught up in a project and don't call for weeks at a time."

Shelby chuckled and shook her head. "So I'm not the only one that you forgot to pick up for a date."

"I swear I didn't mean to hurt you."

"I know. What were you doing that night instead?"

"Breaking into the school's computer system."

Her mouth dropped open. "So the rumors about you changing the grades are true?"

"I broke into the system, but I didn't alter a thing. Sorry to disappoint you."

She eyed him, then asked, "Since we're being completely honest here, did you graffiti the senior rock? Truth."

"Truth?" He swallowed and thought about that night. "The truth is I promised not to divulge what happened then, to protect someone."

"So you didn't do it."

"I didn't say that."

"But you didn't not say it either. You implied you took the fall for someone else."

"I can neither confirm nor deny what you're saying." He whistled through his teeth. "Man, you should have been a lawyer. You would have been a good one." He caressed her neck, noting the soft skin. "There's only thirteen days left until the election. A lot can happen between now and then, but I'm realizing that you'd make a great mayor."

She sneaked a glance at him. "Are you

conceding the race right now? Because I'd be happy to accept and take the mayor's office today."

"No, but what I am saying is that if I have to lose, I'm glad that it's to you."

She let out a breath. "I feel the same way about you. I never would have thought that I'd respect you this much, but the fact that you came to me first with this information about my uncle… It means a lot."

"What are you going to do about it?"

She shrugged and he thought she wasn't going to answer but then she said, "What I have to."

They drove in silence for a while longer, and Josh grappled to continue their conversation. They had just about arrived at the garage when he asked, "Do you have plans Saturday night?"

Shelby looked at him before making the final turn. "Why?"

"I'd rather share the French dinner with you than with my old man. His idea of gourmet is putting Dijon mustard on his hot dog. What do you say?"

"I don't think we should."

"I don't care about what we should do. What do you want to do, Shelby?"

She pulled to the curb in front of her business but didn't answer him. Even in the darkening shadows of the car, he could see the longing in her eyes. "Fine. But we'll eat at my place. It's more private."

He reached over and pushed a strand of hair behind her ear. "I like the sound of that."

"Is it true?"

Laurel paused painting her toenails and frowned at Shelby. "Does it matter? You've already decided it is."

"You made Uncle Bob pressure the officer to drop the charges against you?"

Her sister rolled her eyes. "Made him? I didn't even know he had, until the cop let me out of the jail cell."

Shelby ran a hand through her hair, frustrated. "Laurel, do you understand the position you've put me in here? I'm running for mayor, and yet I'm also sitting on this damaging information about our family."

"Because it's all about you, right?" Laurel returned to applying a bright red polish.

"Why don't you get off your high horse for once and try to understand what life is like for us regular people?"

Harper ran into the living room and jumped into Shelby's lap. "Aunt Shel, would you read me a story?"

Shelby glanced at her watch. "It's after ten, sweetie. A little late for a story." She turned to Laurel. "Shouldn't she be in bed at this hour?"

Her sister rolled her eyes and continued to address her pedicure. "She can sleep in tomorrow, but if you're so concerned, you put her to bed."

Shelby wanted to argue, but where would that get her? Harper wiggled in her lap, so she picked up her niece and carried her into her bedroom. Toys scattered the floor like grenades, and she had to step around them before laying Harper down on the bed. She found a clean nightgown and helped Harper change before tucking the blanket underneath the girl's chin. "Nighty night."

"Don't let the wargles bite."

Shelby gasped. "Wargles? There's wargles in here?" She lifted the blanket and tickled her niece's bare feet. "There they are."

Harper squealed and kicked her legs until Shelby laughed along with her. She sighed and bent to kiss the girl's forehead. "Sleep sweet, my princess."

"Yes, my queen." Harper flipped onto her side and tucked her tiny fist under her chin. When Shelby reached the door and shut the overhead light off, Harper called, "Aunt Shel?"

Shelby turned to look at her. "I'll leave it cracked open. Don't worry."

The girl snuggled farther into the blankets. Shelby returned to the living room where Laurel had finished painting her toes and was twisting the cap back onto the polish. "You can always get her to go to bed without a fuss."

"She should be having regular bedtimes, Laurel. And regular mealtimes. We've talked about this."

"I know. You're a better mother than I am." She waved a hand at the messy room. "And a better housekeeper too, I suppose. Is there anything you can't do?"

"I'm only trying to help you. Mom and Dad have, as well."

"Believe it or not, I don't need your assistance."

"At least until the next get-rich-quick opportunity comes up, and you want a babysitter."

"Speaking of…"

Shelby backed away. "No. I'm on the tail end of the campaign, and it's going to be nonstop from here until then."

"And what am I supposed to do with Harper if—"

"How about putting her first instead of your own selfish wishes? I can't keep dropping my own life to bail you out."

"You owe me."

"No, I don't. I've paid for the accident a thousand times over. And I don't need you rubbing my nose in it anymore."

Laurel pointed to the front door. "Then, get out, because I don't need you telling me what to do or offering help when you obviously won't. I'm perfectly okay, and Harper will be too."

SHELBY TOOK THE papers back from Uncle Bob, who let out a long sigh. "Who else knows about this?"

"Josh Riley. Tim Kehoe."

Her uncle rubbed his forehead. "Which means the whole police force, in other words. I knew it was only a matter of time before this incident was made public."

She couldn't believe she was hearing this. "So, it's true? You convinced the officer not to file the charges?"

"No. I hadn't heard that there had been any charges until the day after the arrest. By then, they'd already been dropped." He looked steadily at her. "You know me, Shelby. I wouldn't use my position to influence an officer to do something."

Shelby pointed to the pages. "But this eyewitness report makes you look like you did."

"Someone obviously wants to put a black mark on me. And our family." He frowned at her. "You don't happen to know anyone who would want to do that, do you?"

"You mean Josh?" She shook her head. "No. Instead of going to the newspaper, he brought this to me. To tell me that he wasn't going to use it to his advantage in the election."

"Do you really think that he won't?"

"I trust him." When her uncle still gazed at her, she insisted, "I do. He's not the same kid that you tried to help go straight, Uncle Bob. He's different now."

"Some leopards can never change their spots."

"So what do you suggest I do? Go to Drew myself to handle this proactively in case Josh does decide to get the information published?"

"I'm saying that you need to prepare a response in the event he does. And your campaign manager would tell you the same thing."

Which is exactly what Mel told her at the bookstore when Shelby shared the material. "We have your uncle's word, so that will help squelch the story. I wonder if we should talk to the officer and get a more accurate statement from him."

"He's left the force. According to my uncle, the choice was not entirely his."

"Then he may have an ax to grind. Great. He probably won't recant any of this statement, despite having the truth on our side."

Shelby took the pages back from Mel.

"There's nothing to worry about. Josh promised that he's not going to use this."

"If he does, it will be in this Sunday's paper in order to make the most damage in time for the election. We should plan to meet that afternoon to discuss our response strategy."

"Mel, you're not listening to me. There's nothing to meet about. He's not going to use this."

"We're talking eleven days to the election. Of course he's going to use it to put him in the lead. Shelby, you need to wake up and understand who we're dealing with here."

"That's the thing. I do see him." She glanced down at her hands. "And he sees me."

Melanie frowned at her words. "What do you mean?" She peered closer into Shelby's eyes. "Are you in love with him?"

She couldn't deny that she was attracted to Josh. That she wondered about a possible future with him. But love? "I don't know."

Melanie rubbed her forehead. "Please tell me that I'm not hearing this. You've fallen for the man you're running against?

I thought that it was a crush that you hadn't outgrown, but it's more serious than I expected."

Shelby wilted onto the stool at the coffee bar. "It's much more than a crush. I meant it when I said that he sees me. More than anyone else, he gets who I really am. And the thing is, he likes the real me."

"Are you saying that me, your best friend for over twenty-five years, doesn't know the real you?"

Shelby paused before she looked away. "You see only what I let you see." She glanced toward the large front window and the display of travel books that graced it. "Did you know I've dreamed about touring Greece? Taking a month off, maybe two, and traveling the whole country?"

"I knew you liked Mediterranean food and that you took that language course."

"But I want to leave Thora. Get away from the pressures that keep me stuck here."

"Stuck here? I thought you loved living here. And you're running for mayor, which will tie you here for the next four more years. Why are you doing this?"

Why hadn't she told all this to Mel before? Because she knew her friend was right. They'd been close since preschool. She saw the tears gathering in Mel's eyes.

That was why. She hadn't wanted to disappoint Mel. Ever. "I should have told you before."

"Yes, you should have." Melanie whirled away from the coffee bar and checked the clock on the wall. "I have to open. You need to go."

"Are you angry?"

"You tell me. I find out my best friend has been keeping secrets from me—"

"They weren't secrets."

"—and this man who has been in her life only a few weeks knows her better than I do? So yes, I'm angry. I've told you about my feelings for Jack from day one." She held up one finger when Shelby started to interrupt. "Day one. I've cried on your shoulder when he dated other girls and got married to Stacey. Then when he got divorced, I shared my hopes with you that he would finally love me. And you always encouraged and supported me. How dare you think that you couldn't share your dreams with me? And that you want to leave Thora?"

"It's more than just that."

Melanie put her hands on her hips. "Clearly I don't know you as well as I thought."

"And this is why I didn't tell you. I didn't want to upset you."

"Since Josh obviously sees you for you, why don't you go find him and tell him all your news? I'm busy."

She stalked to the front door and unlocked it, holding it open for Shelby to leave.

STANDING IN THE middle of the chaos as volunteers made calls and organized signs and pamphlets, Josh hung up his cell phone and held up his hand to Tim. "That was the chief of police. His endorsement of me for mayor is going to be in the Sunday paper."

Tim high-fived the upheld hand. "That's what I'm talking about. It's a new day in Thora."

"He was impressed by my speech about a task force to pair up at-risk youth with police officers in hopes of turning things around early. He wants us to meet next month and set things in motion, whether I triumph or not." Josh typed the information into his phone and couldn't stop grinning.

"But I think that this is really going to happen. I could win this thing."

"You'll nail it, for sure. I guarantee it."

Josh waved off the enthusiasm. "It's early yet, but this will definitely help. It's a step in the right direction."

"Speaking of what you need to win…"

Josh glanced up from his phone and groaned at Tim's expression. "I don't like that face you're making."

"We're going to need more money to keep the campaign going." Tim handed him a sheet of paper that itemized the expenditures over the month since he'd started. "The money we raised helped, but we're going to need a lot more to get the word out. More lawn signs. More mailers. More presence on the internet. And it all costs money."

He knew that running a campaign wouldn't be cheap. "How much more?"

"Five thousand will help. Ten would be better." Tim cocked his head to the side. "Know any rich voters who would like to help support your mayoral bid?"

Not likely. Most of the voters he knew were working hard to keep their families afloat. "Any fundraising we could do in the meantime?"

"Not soon enough to get the flux of cash the campaign needs."

"I've got some in savings that I could use."

"Be sure to report it on the campaign-finance paperwork. I don't want you to be accused of anything unsavory just when you're about to turn this election in your favor."

"You really think this could put me on top? Do I honestly have a chance of beating Shelby?"

"You do if I have anything to say about it."

"I've been thinking about the story you came to me with, about Shelby's sister and uncle."

"I can have it to Drew within the hour."

Josh shook his head. "No. Kill it."

"Josh, we finally have the momentum you need to win, but this will seal the deal. You can't just walk away from the story."

"I gave Shelby my word."

"Who cares? This is politics. She'll understand."

Nobody would, if he let this story get leaked. "I'm not that desperate. And you shouldn't be either." He held up his phone. "The chief of police believes in me. Let's capitalize on that and not pin our hopes on a salacious story that happened years ago."

Tim finally sighed. "Fine. But you're making a huge mistake."

Actually, it felt as if he was on the edge of a victory.

AFTER THE FIGHT with Mel, the idea of a girls' night out with her and Penny didn't appeal to Shelby. She had never argued with her best friend like this. They'd never let days pass without a word before. But she'd promised Penny a night out before she got married, and this evening had been on the calendar for months.

Shelby took a deep breath before knocking on the door to the house her grandparents had once lived in. Christopher answered and smiled. "Come on in. They're waiting for you."

She attempted a cheerful expression and stepped inside. As she followed him into the kitchen, her belly tightened. Reminding herself that this evening was about Penny, she let out a long breath and made her grin wider. "Who's ready for a night of fun?"

Mel turned toward her but didn't smile. Her cousin, on the other hand, rushed forward and hugged her tightly. "I know I am." She let her go and looked between them. "So, what's on the agenda?"

"Someone told me you like that Mediterranean restaurant on Oak." Shelby gave a nod to Christopher. "We'll start there and see where the night takes us."

"And don't forget that we need to pick up Aunt Sarah on the way."

"Yes, I know." Shelby pulled on Penny's arm. "Huh. For someone who accuses me of being bossy, you do a pretty good job of it yourself."

Penny laughed and linked her arm with Mel's too. "I want all my best girlfriends by my side tonight. I may not get to have a full-on bachelorette party because of my crazy work schedule at the station house, but spending time with you all is perfect. Ladies, lead the way!"

They picked up Great-Aunt Sarah at the seniors' home and finished the short walk to the restaurant. When Shelby entered, she gave her name to the hostess, who gave a conspiratorial nod and led them past the rows of tables to a back room. Penny frowned. "I didn't know they had tables back here."

"They must realize it's a special night," Melanie answered and held open the curtain of beads to let Penny enter first.

"Surprise!" twenty women shouted as Penny squealed and clapped her hands.

This time, Shelby's smile was genuine, seeing how happy her cousin was as she took turns hugging each guest. Melanie stood next to her. "You did good."

"We did good." She turned to her. "I hate it when we don't talk. I've been miserable without you." Melanie didn't respond. Instead she joined the rest of the party. Aunt Sarah nudged her. "You two will work it out eventually."

"I need it to be sooner rather than later. We've never fought like this."

"Maybe you should eat a piece of humble pie with dinner tonight." Aunt Sarah gave her a sympathetic look, then moved on to speak to a couple of the other partygoers.

Once dinner had been served and Penny was opening her gifts, Shelby found Mel sitting alone, nursing a glass of wine. She took a seat across the table from her. "I'm sorry that there are things that I haven't told you, but in my defense, I haven't shared them with anyone."

"Except for Josh. Obviously, you can tell him anything."

"He's not my best friend. You are."

Melanie stared at her. "Then why didn't you tell me that you don't want to be mayor?"

"I never said that." And she never had. Hadn't even thought it, at least not seriously. She'd been planning on it for so long that to give up now would be to admit failure. She couldn't, wouldn't do that. "I'm in this race to win it, Mel."

Melanie looked at her, and she felt as if she were a bug underneath a magnifying glass. "Then why does Josh think that you don't want to?"

"I might have mentioned about wanting to escape Thora. To see the world."

"I thought you loved it here."

"I do." Shelby sighed. "But wanting to see something beyond the borders of Thora doesn't make me love it less. I just want more."

Melanie huffed. "It seems like Josh came into your life, and you're changing right in front of my eyes. I thought you were the one person besides Jack who I could depend on to always be there."

"You can still depend on me. That part hasn't changed."

"I'm not so sure. I was always your go-to. I've had your back at every step."

Shelby shook her head. "I know that. And you know that I've got yours. But I can't help it. There's something about Josh. At least, I think there is. But maybe not. Sometimes I'm so confused. This is a mess."

Melanie rose to her feet and came to sit down next to her. "I thought that you didn't want anything more than to win this election. Maybe you need to ask yourself what it is you really want."

Shelby slowed and realized she'd thought of little else. What did she want? To leave Thora? To stay? Did she want to win the election and prove to her family that their expectations of her were justified? Or did she want to find her own path? Perhaps one that took her away from them. This was what now kept her awake at night. Shelby took Mel's hand in hers. "That's what I'm trying to figure out."

"And I'll be right by your side, okay? But no more secrets."

"No more secrets."

They shared a smile when a loud cheer erupted from the group as Penny opened another gift.

SHELBY CHECKED HER watch for the fourth time, then shrugged at the French chef who gave a huff. "If monsieur isn't here in the next five minutes, I'll serve just you. My food can't wait for stragglers."

Shelby agreed and texted Josh again.

Where are you? Dinner's ready.

A dull ache settled in her belly, and she rubbed at it. He wouldn't stand her up. Not again. After all, he'd changed to a man who kept his commitments.

Right?

She drifted to the front window and stared out at the calm street. She'd placed a lot of importance on this meal. Maybe more than she should have, but she wanted to believe that this could be the start of something bigger for the both of them. That this would prove to her that she could stand up for what she wanted, rather than go with her family's expectations again.

"I'll serve you on the patio?"

Shelby nodded. She'd planned this night to take advantage of the romance of a summer evening. Candles and strands of white lights with the sun low on the horizon in the west would provide illumination for their meal. The chef would prepare the food, and she'd placed a speaker on the patio to serenade them with soft jazz.

If only Josh would show.

Shelby was impressed with the patio of her ground-floor condo and took a seat at the special glass bistro table and chairs she'd borrowed from the bakery. The chef set a small plate with escargot in front of her with a flourish before returning inside.

She should have known. Should have expected this from Josh. To keep the moisture in her eyes from falling down her cheeks, Shelby took a deep breath. She would enjoy this dinner and never again let him try to convince her that they could be anything more than what they were. *Friends* was too strong a word. *Colleagues* was close, but *opponents* rang more true to her thinking. He was her opponent, therefore he was her enemy. And she'd be better off to remember that.

A thick onion soup followed the appetizer, and despite the heat of the day, it served to fortify her resolve. The chef raised one eyebrow as Shelby took another spoonful. After swallowing, she stated, "Very good."

"Monsieur Riley said you had no food allergies, right?"

"Yes, that's correct." Her only allergy was to men who promised to be there but then disappeared.

By the time the entrée of lamb chops in a béarnaise sauce was served with tiny roasted potatoes and green bean almandine, Shelby didn't think she could eat another bite. But to appease the chef, she cut off a tiny portion of meat and put it in her mouth, making appreciative noises. It wasn't Simone's fault that the dinner wasn't what it should have been.

A knock on the front door sounded in the distance. Shelby got to her feet and answered it, finding Josh standing on the threshold.

"Sorry I'm late."

She let out a sigh. "I was starting to think that you weren't going to show. What held you up?" She led the way to the patio and took her seat.

Josh slipped into the chair across from her and placed the linen napkin on his lap. "I got involved with a work project and lost track of time."

Shelby dabbed the napkin at the corners of her mouth. "You've missed a wonderful meal."

He pointed at her still-full plate. "Looks like I came in time for the main event." He reached across the table to take her hand, but she withdrew it and placed it in her lap. "I really am sorry. Have I ever stood you up before?" She cocked her head to one side, and he grimaced. "I mean, recently."

Shelby picked up her fork and kept her concentration on the food in front of her.

How did he manage to bring up her adolescent insecurities that she'd struggled with in high school? This was just another reason a relationship between them wouldn't work. If he was a minute late, she'd worry that he wasn't coming. That she wasn't important enough in his life to be a priority.

Simone plunked Josh's dinner before him and huffed back to the kitchen, presumably. Soon the chef appeared with two glasses of wine. She set one in front of Shelby, put a hand on her shoulder and glared at Josh. "I know you brought this with you, but you don't deserve to have any. Standing up this woman who only wanted a nice private dinner with you…" When Josh started to protest, she held up a finger. "You've lost my vote, monsieur."

But she placed the second glass on the table and retreated inside. Shelby took a sip. "It is good wine."

"Let me make this up to you."

"That's just it, Josh. You can't make up time once it's past." She dropped her eyes to her plate. "This whole night was a mistake. I should have listened to my gut when it told me to refuse, but I thought it would be different now."

"It is different."

"If it was, you would have been punctual." Shelby placed her napkin on the table and rose to her feet. "I enjoyed my dinner, and I'll give you that opportunity, as well."

JOSH LONGED TO go after her. Knew he should make things right between them, but she had spoken the truth. If he really meant to pursue something with her, he would have been on time. Should have been. Wasn't his penchant for getting caught up in work what had lost him relationships in the past?

He cut into the lamb chop but felt no joy in the meal. Even the wine, which was good like Shelby had said, gave him no pleasure.

He'd screwed up. Again. Problem was that he'd probably repeat his mistake if his past was any indication.

He wanted a real relationship with Shelby. Wanted it more than he did a new phone app that would possibly fund their future, he hoped. He'd told himself he was working on it for them.

Placing the napkin on the table, he left the patio and searched for Shelby. He found her sitting in the living room with the chef. They both looked up at him when he cleared his throat. "Could I have a moment alone with Shelby?"

"Of course. I have to check on dessert anyway." The chef patted Shelby's hand before glaring at him and leaving the room.

Josh took a seat on the couch next to Shelby, who scooted a few inches away from him. "I know I deserve this, and that you're disappointed in me. I had high hopes for this evening, as well, and I ruined some of that by being late."

"Some?"

"Yes, some. Not all." He shifted closer to her and took her hand in his. "I still have the opportunity to redeem myself tonight but only if you give me the chance to."

"I gave you an opportunity by agreeing to dinner in the first place."

"Fair enough." He scooted even closer. "But what did you think when I was late and not responding to your texts? You assumed that I was standing you up. I had no intention of doing that. I don't call that giving me a chance, do you?"

Shelby bit her lip. Hurt was reflected in her gaze. On the inside, he groaned. He'd upset her, which was the last thing he'd wanted to do. "I am sorry that I was late and I'll do better next time. I promise you that."

"I needed you to do better tonight."

"So let's go back outside and start this evening over. We'll enjoy an amazing French dinner and talk about how we see the future. Our future, if that's what you want." He stood, still holding on to her hand. "Will you do that with me?"

She looked up at him with a watery smile and squeezed his hand. They walked hand in hand out to the patio, and Josh pulled out her chair for her. As she took her seat, he prayed that he wouldn't blow this second chance for the both of them. He brought his chair next to hers and moved his plate and silverware. "Thank you for believing me, Shelby."

She gave a short nod and focused on cutting into her lamb chop. "I do want to try things with you, but I'm scared."

Josh reached over and stilled her hand with his. "I'm scared too."

She lifted her eyes to meet his, a look of surprise on her face. "I thought you were fearless."

"Not when it comes to you." He swallowed the lump of emotion lodged in his throat, acknowledging that was true.

Once their meals were eaten, Simone cleared the table and brought miniature chocolate soufflés that looked decadent, along with coffee served in tiny white cups. Shelby put a hand to her belly. "I don't think I can eat a bite of this, I'm so full."

Josh started to pull her dessert toward him. "Then I'll be happy to eat yours too."

She tapped his hand with her spoon. "Nice try. I don't turn down chocolate."

He smiled back at her and dipped into the soufflé. He closed his eyes as the flavors of the rich dessert seemed to explode in his mouth. Shelby moaned beside him. "I think I've died and been rewarded for all my good behavior."

"If I've died, my bad behavior has been overlooked, then, because this is amazing."

"Did I tell you about the bakery in Athens that lets you take a special dessert-making class while you're there? The chef teaches tourists how to prepare authentic Greek pastries and provides the recipes to take home." Shelby sighed and picked up her cup of coffee. "Can you imagine that? It's like a dream."

"So when are you planning to leave?"

She dropped her eyes to the coffee and stared into its depths. "You know why I can't go."

"If it's money that's stopping you, I can loan it to you."

"No, I have plenty saved up."

"So ask your friend Melanie to go with you. I'm sure she'd agree."

"She would, but that's not stopping me."

"Then what's holding you back?" When she didn't answer but concentrated on eating the soufflé, he said, "Your family won't fall apart if you leave for a few weeks. And neither will the garage. Just go. Make that dream come true."

"I have obligations here. It's not that easy to just pack up and leave."

"Sure it is." He pulled out his phone and

pulled up a search engine for flights to Athens. "They have flights out of Detroit metro daily. When are you going to stop planning this fantasy trip and actually go on it?"

Simone came out onto the patio and stood with her hands clasped before her. "Everything is cleaned up inside, and I've gathered my things, so I'll be leaving."

Josh rose to his feet so he could help her with her supplies, but turned first to Shelby. "I'll be right back."

He followed Simone inside and handed her a few bills. "Thank you for staying."

Simone eyed him warily but tucked the money into her apron pocket. "I did it for her, not you. But you did do the decent thing, not giving up on her or this evening."

He helped the chef to her car, carrying a pair of plastic tubs. Back on the patio, he went to Shelby, standing at the edge of the small yard, staring at the sunset. He walked up behind her and put his hands on her shoulders. She turned into his arms and rested her head on his chest. "Don't make me dream about things that won't happen, Josh."

He tightened his arms around her. "If I had my way, Shelby, I'd give you the whole world, and not just Greece."

CHAPTER NINE

DREAMING OF SHELBY on a Greek beach, Josh groaned as he woke up to the sound of his father slamming open his bedroom door. He rubbed his eyes and propped himself up on one elbow. "Dad?"

His father's cheeks burned almost as bright as his eyes. "You need to pack your stuff and get out of my house."

"Wait. Tell me what's going on."

"I won't have a liar and a cheat living under my roof any longer. That's what's going on. Now, get up and get out."

Maybe he was still asleep, because nothing his dad said made any sense. "Dad, what are you talking about?"

His dad left the bedroom and returned with Thora's Sunday paper and slammed it onto the bed. "You know exactly what I'm talking about."

Josh grabbed the paper and skimmed the

lead article. How had Drew gotten this information about Laurel's charge? "I did not leak this story, Dad. You have to believe me."

"Believe you?" He gave a bark of laughter. "And here I thought you had changed. That you had become the man I always wanted you to be." His father walked to the closet and pulled out one of Josh's suitcases and threw it on the bed. He unzipped it and started slamming clothes into it, hangers and all. "I saw that you were different, but you were fooling us the whole time, weren't you?"

Josh fumbled getting out of bed, but managed to stand and stay his dad's arm. His father shook off his touch and charged back to the closet. Josh blocked his progress, hoping that he could make the old man understand. "But I have changed. Like you said. You've seen it."

"And after you stood there and promised me that you wouldn't hurt Shelby." He opened a dresser drawer with a jerk strong enough to dump the drawer and its contents onto the floor. "I wanted it to be true. I wanted to believe you. And you've made a fool out of me as much as you have of that young woman."

"Dad, listen to me. I didn't do it."

But his father just continued, "When you first left, I told your mother that you needed time and space to grow up. That you couldn't stay a delinquent your whole life. That you needed to mature and that you'd find your path eventually." He opened another drawer and started pulling socks and T-shirts out of it. "She was right though. A bad apple from the beginning. You could never measure up to Joe. Never."

"Stop!"

His father stared at him. His dad's mouth moved, but no words came out of it. Josh stooped and picked up the mess that was on the floor. "Why can't you believe that I told Tim to bury the story, not use it? Do you really believe I'm that horrible of a person?" When his father didn't answer, Josh shook his head. "Of course you do. I've heard it my whole life."

He started to throw the clothes into the open suitcase. "Do you know the words I heard most from you growing up? Not I love you. Or I'm proud of you. But *why can't you be more like your brother, Joe?* And so I tried, but I was never good enough. If I got Bs in school, he got As. If I made the basketball team, he made All State and lettered in three sports. I could never measure up to him."

"That's right. You could never be Joe."

Josh paused folding a T-shirt to look at his father. "I wanted you to see me. To love me for who I was. And when I realized you couldn't, I started doing the opposite of Joe to get your attention. And now I'm back in town, running for mayor so I could hear you say you're proud of me for just once in my life."

"It'll be a cold day when I'm proud of you."

Josh slammed the top of the suitcase down and zipped it shut. "Well, I'm done trying to win your approval. Now I'm going to win that election just for me." He pounded his fist on his chest. "And to show you that I've always been good enough with or without you."

He swung the suitcase off the bed. "I'll be out of your house within the hour. Get out of my room."

HER CELL PHONE wouldn't stop ringing, so Shelby powered it down and placed it on her coffee table as she reread the article for what seemed like the hundredth time. Everyone had been right to warn her about Josh. But she had thought she knew him better than they did. That he wouldn't betray her.

The article proved only that she had been wrong. What had she missed that everyone else had seen? Had she purposely overlooked the signs that he would lie and promise to protect her family?

Tossing the paper away, she turned to stare out the living room window. It looked like it was going to rain again, ruining her family's plans for a barbecue later that afternoon. Not that she really wanted to go anymore. She wasn't looking forward to having to face them and their knowing looks. Or maybe they'd pity her for blindly believing in Josh's change.

She was such an idiot. Hadn't he proved to her who he was when they were in high school? But she'd let his smooth talking and fiery kisses pull the wool over her eyes.

He was probably chuckling over his

morning coffee that not only had he fooled her into thinking that he wouldn't pass along the story but that his path to the mayor's office was now almost guaranteed.

Why hadn't she listened to everyone else? They'd warned her.

Because she had fallen in love with this seemingly new Josh. The one who listened to her and saw through her carefully constructed walls to her authentic self. The one who had held her last night as they dreamed together about a future they might have together once the election was over. Well, it seemed to be over for her now.

A knock on the front door broke into her thoughts, and she pushed herself off the sofa. Her first instinct was to ignore whoever it was, but curiosity won out. She peeked through the peephole.

Josh. What in the world was he doing there?

He knocked again, and she crouched down in case he could see her. She didn't want to see him. Didn't want to hear his excuses. Because there was no excuse. He had looked her in the eye and lied that he wasn't going to use the story.

Well, no more. She would go to Melanie and admit her mistake and together they would craft a response to the front-page story.

"Shelby, your car is here, so I know you're in there. Open the door. I need to talk to you. Please."

Resting the back of her head on the jamb, she stared at the ceiling. "Go home, Josh. There's nothing more to say."

He pounded on the door. "There's plenty to say, and you know it."

Closing her eyes, she decided to wait him out. He'd give up eventually when he realized that she wasn't going to face him.

He continued to knock and even pressed the bell. Five times. Then he stopped, and it got quiet. She checked the peephole, but he still stood there, his head down, almost resting on his chest. "Just leave. I don't want to talk to you."

"Do you really believe that I could do this?" he beseeched her, but she steeled her heart against him. He wouldn't get past the walls around her heart anymore.

But the truth was Shelby didn't answer him because she wasn't sure. She didn't want to believe it, but the evidence seemed to show that he could and had. She'd promised Nana that she'd always protect the family, and the moment she'd stopped to consider what she wanted with Josh instead of what the family wanted, look what had happened to her.

"Please." His voice came out strangled and soft. And looking again through the aperture, she could see his desperation. Was he that good of an actor? She wasn't going to open the door to find out. She couldn't.

Finally, he put his hand on the oak surface, shook his head and walked away. Shelby didn't know if she was relieved or disappointed that he'd given up.

She slowly dropped to the floor and rested her cheek on her knee before letting the tears come.

JOSH LAY ON the bed in the motel room and stared at the ceiling above him. The thump of music in the room next door irritated him, but he didn't have the energy to get off the bed to go ask whoever it was to turn it down.

Shelby didn't believe him. His dad didn't

believe him. Why in the world had he come back to this town anyway? He should have stayed away, even if his dad had needed him. He didn't deserve any of this.

He'd made something of himself in the time away from Thora. And he'd stupidly thought that he could prove himself as the honorable man that he knew he was to his hometown. But you couldn't change history just like you couldn't change people's minds.

He rolled to his side and pulled his knees up almost to his chest. He could get over the fact that Thora's residents might doubt that he was a good man. But it hurt the most that those he loved did too.

Fool that he was, he'd believed that he could convince at least Shelby that she could trust him. That he wouldn't betray her like this. He'd driven to her condo in the hopes that she would listen to his side of the story. But it had been too late. She not only believed he would hurt her like this, but she'd shut herself off from him.

That didn't mean he couldn't keep trying. He pulled his phone from the night stand and texted Shelby again.

You have to believe me. I never said a word to Drew.

He waited, but there was no response to that text or the dozen others he'd sent her since learning about the story that morning.

He didn't know for certain how Drew got the information, but he had an idea. He rolled off the bed and made the call.

TIM MET HIM at the baseball fields where his oldest son was playing. Standing by the chain-link fence that separated the field from the bleachers, Tim waved as Josh approached him. "Did you see the story this morning? This clinches the election for you." Tim looked gleeful at the thought.

But Josh was anything but happy about it. Yes, he wanted to win the election, but not like this. Never like this. "I thought we decided to bury the story."

"You said we should, but I didn't agree."

Josh stared at the man. "Do you realize what this does to my credibility? Everyone is going to think that I leaked it to hurt Shelby's chances in the election."

"And what's so wrong with that? I thought you wanted victory."

Josh clutched the metal fence, unable to believe what he was hearing. "I want to win with honor and grace. Not because my former campaign manager had an ax to grind with my opponent's family."

Tim focused his attention on Josh rather than the game. "Former manager?" He gaped.

"That's right. I don't want you on my campaign anymore. I never wanted to play dirty, and I told you that from the beginning."

"I'm getting you elected. You should be thanking me."

"You're right. I will thank you to stay far away from me and the campaign." Josh shook his head and started to walk away. He turned back for a moment. "I don't need people like you messing around with my reputation or my life. I've made enough of a mess on my own, and I've been trying to pay for my mistakes this whole time."

Tim yelled after him, "You would never have gotten this far without me. Just you remember that."

"Maybe I could have gone further without you! And maybe I still will!" Because this election wasn't over. Not by a long shot. He could still win and keep his integrity. He just had to figure out how.

SHELBY SAT IN her car parked next to the curb, staring up at Christopher's house. The threat of rain had held off, so the Cuthbert family potluck was still on. She wondered if she should have stayed home, like she'd planned, but her mother had left several voice mails begging her to come. So she'd decided to brave her family's pitying looks and offers of support. It didn't matter anymore.

She got out of her car and paused before grabbing the bags of chips she'd picked up at the corner store moments before. She would have been crazy not to notice the looks that she'd gotten from customers as she had stood in line waiting for the cashier. They all stared, but no one uttered a word. The silence spoke more than anything that could have been said anyway.

She straightened and slammed the door. Another vehicle parked behind hers. It was

Uncle Rick and Aunt June arriving. Her aunt exited the car and cocked her head to one side. "Shelby, we read the paper this morning. So, what are you going to do?"

Shelby smiled. "What I always do. Just keep on going."

Uncle Rick put a hand on her shoulder. "That's our brave girl."

Shelby watched them head up the sidewalk to the house. Taking a deep breath, she used it to put steel into her spine and reinforce the walls that she put around her heart. Josh might have thought the story would stop her campaign or even break her. But she was a Cuthbert, after all. And Cuthberts didn't quit.

Even if she wanted to.

Her mom met her at the door and pulled on her arm so that she entered the living room. "I'm so glad you're here. Everything's in chaos, and no one seems to know what to put where. We need your expertise."

"Huh? Salads with salads. Side dishes with sides. Just like always." Was she the only one in the family who could figure this out? Or was her mom giving her a chance to do what she always did. To have some kind of normal in this horrible day. "I'll have everything arranged in a flash."

Her mom searched her eyes. "It can wait a minute. How are you doing?"

Shelby attempted a smile. "Fine."

She peered closer at her, like she had when Shelby had been young and trying to avoid punishment. "How are you really?"

"Mom, I don't want to talk about it here. Everything is going to be okay."

Her mother nodded. "I know, but when someone attacks my baby girl, I tend to worry about her. And want to fight, fight, fight."

"There's nothing to worry about. I'll formulate a response and put the campaign on the right track."

Mom patted her shoulder. "That's my girl."

In the kitchen, conversation stopped when Shelby entered. She looked at their drawn faces and rubbed her forehead. "Listen, I appreciate everyone's concern, but this will all work out. We have the truth on our side, and I'll be sure to get it out there." Still, no one moved. "So let's just enjoy the picnic today and figure out the strategy to-morrow, okay?"

Uncle Mark stepped forward. "She's right, everyone. Our Shelby isn't about to let some upstart stop her campaign. This is a hurdle, that's all."

"A minor one, if I know my girl," her dad said and saluted Shelby with his can of pop.

Conversation changed, and Shelby prac-tically wilted in relief. She concentrated on organizing the food that had been brought but noted that they didn't really need her help. Her mother had been trying to give her a small victory to forget her major de-feat that morning.

Because despite her own words, Shelby knew that she'd suffered a big loss.

An hour later, Shelby could no longer avoid Aunt Sarah, who was moving down the counter, filling her plate. Her great-aunt added a scoop of Aunt June's baked beans as she asked, "I'm guessing you didn't tell Josh how you feel."

Shelby noticed the other family members nearby stop to look at her, seemingly to wait for her answer. Her aunt stayed her hand when she would have placed a spoonful of her mom's potato salad next to her cole-slaw. Shelby looked up at Aunt Sarah and shrugged. "The article in the paper today answers that question. It doesn't matter what I did or didn't say to Josh. It's all over between us now."

She quit the line and took her food outside to the backyard, no longer very hungry. Her aunt followed her. "I thought you were stronger than that. When have you ever shied away from a challenge?"

"When have you? Because I know you haven't talked to Henry. Otherwise, he would be here." Shelby looked around the backyard. "Nope. He's not here, so you didn't summon the courage to do what you're asking of me."

Aunt Sarah pursed her lips. "Henry has nothing to do with this."

"When you get brave enough to talk to him, you can come and lecture me about what I should tell Josh. Until then, I don't want to hear it."

She mumbled an apology and skirted past her aunt. She placed her plate on an empty card table, then pulled out the folding chair. She was soon joined by Penny and Jack, who took seats flanking her. She looked between them. "Don't start with me. I'm not in the mood."

Jack held up his hands. "After the way you talked to Aunt Sarah, I wouldn't dare."

"Then I will." Penny glared at her. "I don't care how much you're hurting over what Josh did to you, but you don't dare take it out on Aunt Sarah. She has been nothing but supportive to all of us. And if you ever speak to her like that again, you will answer to me."

Shelby paused from unrolling the napkin that held the plastic utensils. She hadn't meant to lash out like she had. And she'd regretted the words as soon as they were said. But that didn't change the fact that she hurt too. And no one seemed to understand. They all acted as if she should have known that her heart would get broken by Josh and should get over it. But the article this morning had blindsided her. "Are you finished?"

Penny's mouth was set in a tight grimace. "The question is, are you?"

Shelby knew that Penny was right. "With Aunt Sarah? Yes. I said I was sorry, but I'll apologize again, properly, to her later." She arranged her plate and sighed. "With the election? Maybe I'm wrong, and I should quit now and try to salvage what's left of our family's reputation. I promised Nana that I would always protect the family, but it looks like I've failed her."

"You can't drop out, Shel. You gotta be brave." Jack peered at her. "Josh pulls out this story at the last minute, and you're going to roll over and let him get away with it? That doesn't sound like you."

"He claims he didn't leak the information."

"And you believe him?"

She had. She'd looked into his eyes and believed that he believed in her. She put a fist to her forehead. "I don't know anymore. I thought I knew him, but I was wrong. So wrong." She used her napkin to dab at her eyes. "I'm surprised that Laurel isn't here to say I told you so."

"She'd never do that, Shel. She's upset, but give her time. I'm sure you two will work things out."

Shelby nodded at Jack's words. "And what should I do about the election? Any statement I make now will sound like I'm trying to spin it. And most people will have made up their minds about what happened."

Penny grabbed her hand. "You're going to have Drew print the truth about what really happened. It's like you said. We have the facts on our side."

"Even if he agrees to do it, the next edition isn't out until next Sunday, which is two days before the election. It's too late by that time."

"Then you spread the information another way. Call Melanie and figure this out." Jack handed her his cell, but Shelby wasn't sure if she could, remembering the last time she'd talked to her friend. He sighed and pressed it into her hand. "Call her."

Shelby took the phone and stared at it before looking up at her cousins. "Thanks. I knew I could count on you both." She stood and punched in Mel's number as she walked toward the back fence line. The phone rang twice. "I'm on my way with the fruit salad. Promise. I got caught up in this book I'm reading and lost track of time."

"It's me. Jack let me borrow his cell." Mel fell silent on the other end. Shelby let a few moments pass before she said, "You were right about Josh, and I should have listened to you. He was using me this whole time."

Still nothing from Mel. Desperate to fill the silence, Shelby rushed her words. "You were right. I was wrong. Please forgive me."

"I will, but only if you forgive me too."

The apology was whispered and brought tears to Shelby's eyes. She wiped them away, nodding, although Mel couldn't see her. "Always."

"Maybe I didn't want to see what Josh has seen in you all along. Because if you're not happy here, you'll leave me. And that would be the worst thing besides losing Jack."

"I promise that you're not going to lose me."

"And I promise to support you and whatever space you need to be happier." Mel took a deep breath. "Now, what are we going to do about this article concerning your sister? And how do we counter Chief Winter's endorsement of Josh? We need something big to turn this around."

CHAPTER TEN

THE LAST PUSH to the election was on, and Josh scheduled several appearances at local businesses in order to drum up support. Without Tim to make the arrangements for him, he found himself scrambling to take care of the details. He wanted to turn the tide of negative publicity that both campaigns had received with Sunday's article. He hoped winning would prove that he was an honorable man, after all.

At the car wash, he dried vehicles as they exited. At the bakery, he bought doughnuts and cups of coffee for the customers. At Ted's Diner, he served as a waiter on Tuesday night, a week before the election, to help raise money for the local Special Olympics chapter. But changing his image seemed to be impossible.

And he was definitely missing Shelby.

He wanted her trust. Her forgiveness. But he wanted her love most of all.

He wished she could have believed him. Had he not proven that he was changed? That he could be the man of integrity that she wanted? But she'd rejected him. And while he might miss her, he couldn't let his feelings for her make him forget that he really was a good person. Her opinion of him wouldn't make that any less true.

But it certainly wouldn't help either.

Aunt Sarah flagged him down. She was sitting with an older fellow he recalled meeting at the seniors' center the day of his speech. "Have you both decided what you want to order?"

Sarah looked across the table at her companion. "Henry, what do you feel like?"

The man looked at Josh. "When I was a young man like you, they used to serve an ice-cream sundae with scoops of all the ice-cream flavors and covered in all the toppings. They still got that here?"

"The Big Pig? They sure do."

Henry smiled at Sarah. "What do you think? For old times' sake?"

Sarah smiled too and nodded. "You always had a sweet tooth. I see that hasn't changed." To Josh, she said, "One Big Pig and two extra-large spoons."

"Coming up right away." Josh was about to go and prepare the dessert but turned back to Sarah. "Have you heard from Shelby?"

"You mean, since the article came out?" The older woman said softly, "She's not happy with you. Or Drew, for that matter. Why didn't he try to get a statement from her? Or Bob since he's the one who looks guilty."

"I didn't leak that story."

Aunt Sarah paused, then nodded. "I probably shouldn't, but I believe you. The article may win you the election, but you lose Shelby in the process, and I'm wagering that's the last thing you wanted."

"She won't take my calls. I showed up at her front door, but she wouldn't open it. I don't know what else to do."

When Aunt Sarah started speaking, Henry put a hand on hers. "Dearest, why don't I take this one?"

Aunt Sarah grinned and squeezed Henry's hand. "But I get the chance to offer a rebuttal."

Henry returned the smile, then faced

Josh. "Women need more than just words. They need action. A big gesture. Especially if it shows them how much you care."

Josh looked between the two senior citizens. "What did you do, Henry?"

Henry scoffed. "Ah, you don't want to hear that story." But he seemed to wait for Josh to insist before continuing. "I had the seniors' home director play our song over the intercom system last night at suppertime. Then I entered the dining room wearing my best three-piece suit, with a pocket handkerchief, and carrying one stem of her favorite flower."

Sarah blushed, smiling warmly at Henry. "I can't believe you remembered I love tulips."

"And you know how hard it is to find those in the dog days of summer?" Henry reached across the table and took Sarah's hand in his. "But I realized that to win back your heart you needed to understand how dedicated I was. I wasn't going to let another day pass without you. And if I had to find tulips at the end of July in Siberia, I would move heaven and earth to find one for you."

Josh noted how the two of them gazed into each other's eyes, and he wondered if he would get the chance to do that with Shelby one day.

But more than just one day. All of their days, until they were in their eighties and coming to the diner to order a Big Pig to share.

If only he could figure out the grand gesture that would show Shelby how much he cared about her.

Aunt Sarah proclaimed, "Henry's right, Josh. And if you love Shelby like I think you do, you'll figure this out." She cocked her head to one side and smiled. "You know, she's holding a press conference at noon tomorrow at the garage to address the story. In case you're interested in attending."

THIS PRESS CONFERENCE had to work. It was her last-ditch effort to get the voters believing her. Shelby smoothed the front of her suit jacket as Uncle Bob approached. "You ready for this, kid?"

"Jack was right. We can't wait until the next edition of the newspaper to tell our side of the story." She reached up and straightened his tie. "What about you? Are you ready?"

Uncle Bob winced at her. "My only regret is that this hurt your campaign."

"That's why we're here. To fix the damage."

Melanie came up alongside them. "Drew is also here, as well as members of the Detroit press. I warned him that he needs to give both sides of the story this time if he wants to keep his credibility intact in this town. So it's important that we emphasize the facts of this case."

"We know, Mel." Uncle Bob patted her shoulder. "I've been to enough of these when I was police chief to understand what's at stake."

Melanie waved them toward the entrance of the garage where the press waited. She'd told Shelby that she wanted the public to see her on her home turf. From a place of strength rather than retreat. That's why she wore a suit in a dark navy shade. Tough but fair, and in the earnest pursuit of truth. Because that was what they had on their side of this story.

Shelby greeted everyone and thanked

them for coming. She saw Josh standing at the edge of the group. It had been three days since he'd come knocking on her door. More than seventy-two hours since he'd blown up her phone asking for a chance to explain. She took a deep breath and let it fortify her. "In six days, the voters of Thora will decide who will be the next mayor. A recent story that was published—" here, she looked straight at Drew, who paled at her scrutiny "—questioned my family's integrity and thus my own. My uncle Robert Cuthbert, chief of police at the time of the incident and now retired, is here to set the story straight."

As her uncle laid out the facts of Laurel's arrest and the subsequent dropping of the charges, Shelby allowed herself to peek at Josh. He appeared haggard, as if he hadn't gotten any more sleep than she had. It looked like he hadn't shaved in days, but the scruffy appearance seemed to suit him.

Closing her eyes, she reminded herself that this was the same man who had tried to torpedo her election chances. She shouldn't still be finding him attractive or being concerned that he wasn't taking care of himself. Those things didn't matter anymore.

"I'd like to address the issue of the leaking of the story."

She opened her eyes to find Josh coming forward. He kept his eyes on hers until he turned to face the press. "It's come to light that my campaign manager investigated and gave the details of the story, without my knowledge or consent, to the local paper. And he has been subsequently fired from my campaign. It was never my intention to hurt Ms. Cuthbert or her family." He turned to look at her, his eyes burning. "I want to sincerely apologize to them for what happened."

Shelby's mouth dropped open. He didn't have to apologize so publicly. It could hurt his own election chances by doing this, but he didn't seem to care. She felt her breath catch in her throat and wanted to put her arms around him. To talk to him as he'd been wanting to do, been asking to do for days. But she gave him a nod, after which he turned on his heel and left.

There were a few questions from the

press, but they had their story and soon dispersed.

"Did you know he was coming here?" Melanie asked her. Shelby shook her head as Melanie whistled softly. "That took a lot of courage. He didn't have to do that." She put a hand on Shelby's arm. "Maybe I was wrong about him, after all."

Shelby noticed him heading for his truck. "I'll be right back." Then she ran after him before he could leave.

She caught up with him just as he started the engine. She went to the driver's-side door and knocked on the window. He saw her but didn't roll it down. "Why did you come here today?" she asked.

He kept his eyes on hers and finally lowered the glass. "I needed you to know the truth."

She gripped the frame where the window had been. "You didn't have to do that."

"Yes, I did."

"Why?"

He looked straight at her. "Because I need you to believe in me. None of this will matter if you don't."

He started to close up the window, so she

removed her hand. Josh gave her a nod, then backed out and drove away.

THE KNOCK ON his motel room door made him turn his head away from the baseball game that played on the television. He reached for the remote and lowered the volume before swinging his legs off the bed and answering.

His father stood there. Josh looked at him, then scanned the street. "How did you find me?"

"Roy is married to Trudy, who works here. She might have mentioned to him that you were staying here." His father glanced behind him. "May I come in?"

Josh stood back and waved his father inside before closing the door. "What do you want?"

His father pointed at the television. "Who's winning?"

"Dad…"

His father dropped his gaze to the floor. "This isn't easy for me."

"What isn't?"

He raised his eyes to look into Josh's. "Apologizing."

Josh felt as if he were on a carnival ride and the floor had dropped away. He stared at his father. "What did you say?"

His father cleared his throat and looked at a spot on the wall behind Josh. "I'm sorry that I assumed that you leaked the story." He shifted his weight from one foot to the other and waved his arms. "There. I said it. Now, pack your things and move back home."

His father said the simple words as if that was all that was needed, but Josh knew he was wrong. "Dad, it's going to take a lot more than saying you're sorry for that to happen." He put his hands on his hips. "Why did you think I would leak the story in the first place?"

"Because I didn't know better."

"No, Dad. Because you didn't know me." He tapped his chest. "I've been back more than six months, but you haven't taken the time to understand who I am now. You spend more time with the television set than you do with me."

"And you're on your phone all day."

Josh nodded. "I'll admit that, and that I'm not perfect in this relationship either. I could have made more of an effort with you too. But this has got to be a two-way street for this to work."

"Sure, sure, we'll spend a bunch more time together. Now, pack."

"I can't move back in with you."

His dad's mouth hung open. "But I said I was sorry."

"Why do you want me to live with you? All you did was complain that I was on your back about watching your diet and taking your meds."

"Because..." His old man blinked a few times and looked away. "It's too quiet in the house without your mother."

"And?"

He looked at him. "And I miss you. Even with your nagging."

Well, it was definitely something. More kind and honest words than his father had ever said to him before. "No. I can't live with you just because you're lonely and need a nursemaid. You could hire someone to take care of you for that."

"But they wouldn't be my son." His father took a step forward. "You're the only kin I have left, Josh. And blood has to stand for something."

"But I'm not Joe, and I never will be."

"Can I sit down?"

Josh helped his father perch on the edge of the bed and took a seat next to him. They both watched the baseball game for a moment. When his father spoke, it was hushed, so soft he almost missed it. "When your brother died, I felt as if my whole world was buried along with him. And I wanted to mold you into a copy of him. That way I wouldn't lose him completely, if you did exactly what he did. But you were nothing like him."

"Dad…"

"I was wrong to try." His father took his hand in his. "It was only after you left Thora that I realized that I'd messed it all up. Now I haven't lost just Joe, but you too. And your mother never forgave me." He looked up into Josh's eyes. "That's why I need you to move back home. To give us the chance we never had to be the father and son I would like us to be."

Josh swallowed at the lump in his throat

as he squeezed his father's hand. "You haven't lost me."

"So you'll come back home?"

"I'll think about it."

They turned back to the game. At the next commercial, Josh let out a long pent-up breath. "I've thought about it. And I have some conditions before I'll agree."

His father eyed him. "Like what?"

"First, you don't complain about eating your vegetables. I'm not making them just for my own benefit. They're good for you."

His dad sighed. "Okay. Anything else?"

"You'll take your medications as prescribed. And no hiding them to make me think you took them." Josh cleared his throat. "If we're going to get to know each other again, I need you to be around for a long time. Got it?"

"Sure. What else?"

"Lastly, we're going to do things together."

"Like what?" His dad appeared wary of this condition.

"Bowling. Go to the movies. Walks around the neighborhood. It doesn't matter. I want us to spend time with each other."

His dad agreed and rubbed his upper lip. "You know, I was a good bowler back in the day. Your mom and I used to belong to a league. I'm pretty sure I've still got the skills and can beat you easy peasy, boy."

"I'd like to see you try."

The two men shared a smile. Josh stood. "So, are you going to help me pack or what?"

Can we talk face-to-face?

SHELBY HAD SENT the text over an hour ago, but still no response from Josh. Not that she had really expected one. Hoped, maybe, but hadn't assumed that he'd answer. She knew she'd hurt him and it was going to take more than a few texts to make it up to him. It had been a few days since the press conference, and she'd taken the time to do some thinking.

What if he hadn't leaked the story, after all? What if he could have been what he claimed to be all along, but she'd been too scared to believe the truth, when it appeared otherwise? She'd been holding his past against him. Putting that between them, along with the election and her family's expectations. What if she set all of that aside to see if the future they had talked about last Saturday night could really happen?

She checked her phone again just in case he had responded and she hadn't noticed. Nothing. Maybe Aunt Sarah was right and that she should draw some courage to talk to Josh honestly and frankly. She swallowed and found his name in her directory, then pressed talk. It rang five times, and she waited for his voice mail message to begin. Instead, she heard Josh himself. "I can't talk right now, Shelby. I'm in the middle of something with my dad."

He still sounded upset with her. "Oh. I can call later."

The sound on the other end of the call muffled for a second. Then he was back. "Can you give me an hour? I'll meet you wherever you want."

She hung up with a promise to phone in an hour with a place where they could meet privately. She flopped back onto her bed and stared up at the ceiling. It really could use a fresh coat of paint. Actually, the whole condo could use a refresh, but she'd put it off with plans to move. Eventually.

That was the problem. Everything she wanted was put off to *eventually*, but that time never seemed to arrive. Her responsibilities to others always came first, and she stayed where she was instead of taking a chance on a different future. Whether it was a family event, a committee she led or obligations to her employees and friends, she had more time for everyone else than herself. Anything she wanted for herself came at the bottom of the list.

Her phone rang. It was her sister. "I'm not available to babysit tonight, Laurel. I've got plans."

"Shel, Harper drank some of my iced tea, and it's like she fell asleep. I can't wake her up."

Her sister sounded frantic, but she often used that tactic to get Shelby to do what she wanted. "I'm sure it's fine. She's probably just tired."

Laurel paused. "I didn't have just tea in that glass."

Shelby sat straight up, knowing what her

sister had probably added. "Hang up with me and call 9-1-1."

"I'll maybe lose her. I can't. You need to come fix this."

"Laurel, hang up and call 9-1-1, or I swear, I'll do it myself."

"All…all right. But please come. I need you."

Shelby slipped her bare feet into a pair of sandals before snatching her purse off the kitchen table and hurrying out the front door. She reached Laurel's apartment in record time and could see the paramedics running inside. Shelby followed them and found Laurel sitting on the floor with Harper's head in her lap. The girl looked ghastly white.

"What did she take, ma'am?" one of the paramedics was asking.

Laurel pushed Harper's bangs off her forehead. "She drank some of my iced tea with a bit of gin mixed in." Her sister paused before adding, "And some pain pills that I had crushed up."

The paramedic paused, and his partner kneeled down and started pulling things out of her bag. She started an IV on Harper, producing more plastic tubing from the bag. A seizure started to shake the little girl violently. Pushing Laurel out of the way, the paramedic inserted the tubing into Harper's throat. The little girl coughed and began to cry.

Laurel stood and grabbed Shelby's hand, watching her little girl shake. "She's gotta be okay. She just has to be."

The first paramedic lifted Harper on to a gurney and began to leave the apartment. Laurel ran up behind him. "I'm going with you."

He gingerly carried Harper to the waiting ambulance. Laurel followed and jumped into the back of the vehicle to be next to her daughter. Shelby still felt a sense of panic. "Where will they take her?" she asked the other paramedic, but she had run after her partner and didn't answer.

Pushing away the anxiety and worry for a second, she realized she knew the answer anyway. Shelby shut the apartment door behind her and bolted for her car. Once she was inside, she pulled her cell phone out of her purse and called her parents, who agreed to meet her at the emergency room of Thora Medical.

Once Shelby arrived, she checked in at the admin desk and took a seat in the lobby. Her mother was the first to enter and she rushed over to Shelby. They hugged tightly before her mom looked into her eyes. "What happened?"

Shelby told her what details she knew and repeated them when her father joined them. He sagged onto a plastic chair and put his head in his hands. Shelby sat next to him, her mother on his other side, her hand rubbing his back. What would it be like to face this crisis with someone by her side? And not just anyone, but Josh. To be able to lean on him when the fear threatened to overtake her.

Instead, she wrapped her arms around her middle and stared straight ahead at the hall that led to the trauma center. Closing her eyes, she wished that she could go back and protect Harper from this happening. But then, she'd never thought her sister would be so careless. Tears squeezed out from behind her eyelids, and she sniffed as she used the back of her hand to wipe them away. Careless or not, her sister hadn't meant for it to happen. But Harper was paying the price.

Her phone rang, and she glanced at the screen. Josh. She stood. "I'll be right back," she told them. "I gotta take this."

She stepped outside into the heat and sheltered her eyes from the bright sun. "Something's come up. I can't meet with you today." Silence on the other end. And she knew she'd said the wrong thing. She took a deep breath. "I'm at the hospital right now."

"Are you okay?"

The concern in his voice warmed her. "It's my niece." She didn't share the details with him. Couldn't share them because a little part of her was still unsure if she could trust him after everything that had happened. Would he go to Drew with the story? Use it against her?

She paused. No, he wouldn't. Hadn't he proven to her that not only had he not leaked the story about her uncle but that he was willing to set the record straight even if it hurt his own chance to win the election?

"Is she going to be okay?"

Shelby bit her lip and shrugged, even though she knew he couldn't see her. Tears strangled her voice. "I don't know."

"Which hospital are you at?"

She told him. "But you can't come, Josh. My family's here."

"So? I'm coming to see you, not them."

"That's not a good idea."

"I don't care. I'll be right there." And he was gone.

She stared at the phone and then glanced over her shoulder at the entrance to the emergency room. She needed to go back inside to be with her family, but her need to see Josh warred with that. He could be here in minutes, and what could she do inside but wait in a chair until Laurel came out with news?

"Shelby?" She turned to find her mother standing in the entrance. "There's been an update."

JOSH DROVE HIS TRUCK, cursing at the red lights and fellow drivers who blocked his path from getting to Shelby sooner. She needed him. He could hear it in her voice.

And he would move heaven and earth if he had to in order to reach her.

He pulled into the hospital's parking lot, took the first available spot and ran to the emergency room entrance. He'd spent enough time in the ER growing up, when poor Joe had been sick, but it looked as if changes had been made since he'd last been there. Brushing aside those thoughts to concentrate on Shelby and the here and now, he sprinted through the electronic doors to scan the lobby. Shelby sat hunched over in a plastic chair, her hands covering her eyes. He knelt before her, putting a hand on her knee. "I'm here."

Shelby looked up at him, then crushed him into a tight hug. "Oh, Josh. I'm so worried."

He instantly wrapped one arm around her waist as her tears dampened his shoulder. He put his free hand on the back of her head, holding her close.

Shelby sniffled and started to back away from him, but he couldn't let her go. He might have come home to take care of his father, but this woman in his arms was the reason he would stay. She had become his purpose. If only he could make her see that.

Shelby's tears subsided, and Josh took the chair next to hers, keeping her hand in his. With halting words, she told him about her niece. "She's unconscious, and the doctor doesn't know when she'll come out of it. She said we have to wait and see."

Josh ran his thumb over hers, wishing he could offer her more than that simple gesture of comfort. "I'm sure they're doing everything they can."

Shelby sat back in her chair and let go of his hand. He didn't need to look to know that her parents must be watching them. Were they surprised? Angry? They had made no bones about not liking him when he'd been a teenager and hadn't made him feel very welcome since he'd returned to Thora. Josh didn't care. The woman he loved needed him.

He paused. The woman he loved. He reached over and used his thumb to wipe away a tear that clung to Shelby's eyelash. "What do you need me to do?"

"Thank you for coming, but you should go home. There's nothing you can do."

"We have to only be honest with each other from now on, Shelby." He settled back into the chair because he knew that's what she wanted him to do. Especially with her parents watching them.

Shelby settled against him, sighing as if his choice to stay had been inevitable.

He rubbed her bare arm, then acknowledged her parents. Her mother seemed shocked by his presence while her father frowned at him. "Mr. and Mrs. Cuthbert."

"Josh," her father answered with a jerk of his head that might have been a nod.

Her mother glanced at her husband, then back at Josh. "How long have the two of you been seeing each other?"

"We haven't." Her mother stared at him as if she didn't believe him. "We've been too busy campaigning against each other."

"But it seems you found some common ground. Maybe there was more to that kiss on the front page than you led us to believe."

Shelby lifted her head. "Mom. Not now."

Her mother sniffed and crossed her arms. "Just don't expect me to approve."

Her father placed a hand on her mother's

shoulder. "This isn't the time for this discussion, Anna."

He felt as if he needed to do something. Anything that might help Shelby. "There's got to be a vending machine or cafeteria around here, and it's probably going to be a long night. Can I get you something?"

Shelby requested a coffee, and he turned to her parents. "Mrs. Cuthbert?"

The woman shook her head, so he asked her father, who rose to his feet. "I'll walk to the cafeteria with you, Josh."

Josh pressed a kiss to the top of Shelby's head and followed her father from the waiting room. The cafeteria was located on the second floor, and they discovered the place was about to close. Josh poured a coffee for Shelby and one for himself, then held up an empty cup to her father. "Interested?"

Mr. Cuthbert leaned on the counter and regarded him. "What exactly is going on between you and my daughter?"

"I thought this wasn't the time for that discussion."

"In the middle of a lobby where everyone can hear? No, that wasn't the time. But now it's just the two of us. And when it involves my daughter, I would like to know."

"Are you asking me my intentions toward her?"

Mr. Cuthbert took the empty coffee cup and filled it from one of the carafes on the warming plates. "Shelby is in a vulnerable place right now. And I don't mean just because of Harper." He put a drop of cream in his coffee. "She really wants to win this election. It's something she's been working toward for a long while, and I'm not going to let you stand in her way."

"If that's what Shelby really wants, I'm not the one in her way."

Her father frowned at him. "What do you mean, *if*?"

Josh realized he'd stepped into territory he should have left alone. "I just meant that Shelby has a way of pursuing what she wants. If that's the mayor's office, she'll get there."

"You said *if* again. Are you saying that she doesn't want to win?"

He added cream to Shelby's coffee and took his time stirring it, hoping that her father would drop the direction of this conversation. Josh wasn't sure her dad would like the answer. "We should get back," Josh told him.

Her father stayed where he was. "Do you think you understand my daughter better than I do? Better than her mother does? Because believe me, Josh, you don't know anything."

"I know more than you think."

Mr. Cuthbert strode to the registers and insisted on paying for all the drinks before walking quickly from the cafeteria, leaving Josh to trail after him.

HARPER WAS STABLE, so she was moved from the emergency room to the ICU, and the doctor recommended that Laurel and the rest of the family go home and get some rest, to which Laurel plunked into the chair beside Harper's bed and refused to leave until her daughter woke up. Shelby offered to retrieve some things for her from home.

As she and Josh walked out of the hospital, he put his arm around her shoulders. "Are you going to be okay?" he asked.

She stopped at her car and looked up at him. "Why did you come here tonight?"

He put a hand on her cheek. "Because you needed me and I couldn't stay away."

Shelby took a step back. She'd seen the tension between Josh and her dad. Whatever they'd talked about had not been pleasant. "I should go get those things for Laurel."

"Shelby, why are you acting like this?"

"I need to go. I appreciate that you came here tonight to check on me—"

"That's not why I came."

"—but don't read more into it than what's really there."

Josh looked stunned. "And what is really there? Why don't you say what you're actually thinking, Shelby? That you're scared of what's going on, so you want to put up this wall between us."

"But that's just it, Josh. The wall has always been there. We can't be together."

"The election will be over in three days. And then—"

"Then, what? You and I are going to date?" Shelby shook her head. The idea seemed ludicrous now. "That's never going to happen."

He frowned at her. "You seem so certain."

"I can't be with you."

"At first, I thought it was our history, but we got past that. And we have the election coming up, but it will soon be decided. So what is it that's really keeping us apart? Your family?"

"They don't approve of you."

"In my experience, most parents don't." He put his hands on his hips. "You're going to let them keep us apart even after the election?"

"My family means everything to me."

"What about what you want?"

"I don't want to hurt them. They expect me to do what is right."

"That's not what I asked you." He pleaded his case, and Shelby was desperate to tell him she loved him and be held again in his arms. Instead, she looked away. "What do you want?"

You.

But she couldn't have him without her family's acceptance. Couldn't he see that? "I have got to go. Laurel's waiting for her things."

Josh yielded and took a step toward his truck. "I really do understand, but let's be clear. I want the same thing as you. And it doesn't matter if your family or mine supports the idea. What counts is you and me and what we feel about each other."

He left and Shelby watched him go, regretting that she wasn't brave enough to tell him how she really felt.

LATER THAT EVENING, Shelby returned to the hospital with a bag of clothes and personal items for Laurel. At the ICU, Shelby checked in with the nurse, asking her to let her sister know she was there. Walking to the waiting room, she hoped that Harper had woken up while she'd been gone. She took a seat in a wooden chair with a thin cushion and placed the bag at her feet. Her aunt Jeri nodded at her as she worked her knitting needles in a quick rhythm.

Laurel entered and Shelby noted that her sister was calm and in control, albeit still upset. She gave Shelby a quick hug and took the seat next to her. "Thanks for doing this."

"Any change?"

Laurel closed her eyes, wincing. "This is all my fault."

"How did she get a hold of your drink?"

"I was making dinner and wasn't paying attention. She's never tried to drink out of my glass before, so I didn't anticipate it or anything."

"How long has the drinking and using been going on?"

Laurel rose and stared at Shelby. "This isn't about me. This is about my little girl's life." She pointed toward the ICU.

"You just admitted that it was your fault."

"Not the way you say it. Like I'm some junkie."

"Aren't you? You've gone back to using again and mixing it with alcohol." Shelby reached out a hand. "You need help, and I will keep offering and offering, no matter how many times before you'll believe what's happening and agree. That little girl in that room, as you said, needs a healthy mom, but that's not what she's got right now."

Laurel stared at her before her face crumpled. "A police officer came earlier to question me. And child services had to be called. They've started an investigation on me." She wrapped her arms around herself. "I admit I'm not the perfect mom, but I would never harm Harper. You know that."

"But she got hurt tonight, just the same."

Laurel snatched the bag at Shelby's feet. "I asked you to get me my things, not to lecture me about what a horrible mom you think I am. This is not the time for this."

"Then when is the time? When you've been drinking and driving and get in an accident? Do you want to carry the guilt of something that could hurt your daughter for the rest of her life and yours?"

"I'm not the one carrying that guilt. That's you."

"I wasn't drinking that night when you were hurt. I was completely sober, but the roads were icy. I lost control of the car. It was an accident. It was not my fault."

"And I'm the one who suffered."

"But tonight wasn't an accident. You can control whether you're drinking or not… and the pills." Shelby stared into her sister's eyes. "Can't you?"

Laurel stared back at her but eventually glanced away. "I need to go back in and stay with her."

When her sister started to leave, Shelby

grabbed her arm. "This is your wake-up call, Laurel. Don't ignore it."

Laurel snatched her arm away and stalked out of the room.

SUNDAY MORNING CAME too early. Josh flopped onto his back and tried closing his eyes, his arm draped over his forehead. Something had woken him. Probably the dream he'd been having about Shelby. They'd been standing on the edge of a lake, the waves lapping at their bare feet. Suddenly, he plunged into the cold water, then turned and held out his hand to Shelby to join him. But she'd stayed safely on the shore while the waves got larger, threatening to drown him if he didn't swim either toward the strand where Shelby was or take a chance pushing past the waves to where he knew something better waited.

A psychologist didn't have to try to explain what the dream meant. Shelby's words last night echoed in his brain. She couldn't be with him because her family's approval and expectations for her came first in her world. While he might be able to flout what other people wanted of him, Shelby never had. To refuse them would be to plunge into the waves with him and try to find safety farther out. Even if he wanted her to choose him, he wanted her to do so under her own steam. He'd never push her to face a decision like that.

A soft knock on the bedroom door alerted him that his father was up. "I'm awake, Dad."

His father opened the door and took a small step forward. "You didn't get in until late last night. Everything okay?"

Josh sat up on the side of his bed, staring at his legs. "I went for a drive to think over some things."

"This about the election? Or about Shelby?"

Josh nodded slowly. "Both. I have feelings for her, and none of this will mean anything if I can't be with her."

His dad's eyebrows disappeared into his hairline. "I thought this was just a crush."

"Part of me hoped it was. That it would be something I could get over, and life would go back to normal." He rose to his feet and crossed the room to his dresser, looking at himself in the mirror. "But I can't get over her that easy. Turns out my emotions run pretty deep." He faced his dad. "I dream about her and I being together and raising a family. How crazy is that? I've never even entertained the idea of something like that with any other woman."

His dad whistled. "Sounds like you're serious about her."

"I am. But I keep going back to the same thought. How can I win the election and not lose her?"

"I guess you'll have to decide which one is more important to you."

Josh agreed with his father. He knew that he could make a difference in Thora by leading it to a more secure financial future. But he also knew that the achievement would feel empty without Shelby by his side. "The election is two days away. It's too late to pull out now."

"Then maybe the question really is how can you have both?"

Josh nodded. "That's what I've been trying to figure out. Any ideas?"

His dad shrugged. "Maybe. You willing to listen?"

"I'm willing to do whatever it takes."

SHELBY PLACED COINS into the vending machine and pressed the button for a French vanilla cappuccino. She quickly placed the cup under the spout, waiting for her drink.

"Got any more of those quarters?"

She turned to find her dad leaning on the wall behind her. She held up her wallet. "Always prepared. Isn't that what you taught me?"

Once her drink had been poured and set aside, she put more coins in and pressed the button for regular brew. None of that frou-frou coffee for her dad. He liked it hot and black. Nothing fancy. It didn't even have to be good, if the kind at the garage was any indication.

They took their coffees to the waiting room, where her mom stood and waved them over. "Harper's waking up, and the doctor thinks she's going to be okay. They have to run tests to be sure, but it looks like she's out of the woods."

Shelby smiled and hugged her dad tightly before putting her arms around her mom. "Thank goodness."

"I'm going to go in and see her. Will you two be okay here?"

Her dad gestured at the empty room. "I think we'll be fine here, Anna."

Her mom stood on tiptoe to kiss his cheek before leaving. Her dad waved his hand at a seat. "Might as well get comfortable. She could be in there for a while."

They sipped their drinks, the drone of a television broadcasting news in the corner the only sound to break the silence. Shelby closed her eyes, grateful that her niece had finally woken up.

"Laurel's agreed to go to rehab."

She opened her eyes to peer at her dad. "I wasn't sure she would. How did you get her to agree?"

"I didn't. She approached me. Someone must have said something to convince her."

Shelby tried to hide her smile. She was so happy and grateful she'd gotten through to her sister. Her father continued, "I found an inpatient facility a couple hours north of here. As soon as Harper is stabilized, I'll take her there myself."

"What about Harper?"

"Your mom and I talked about it. She'll stay with us until your sister is firmly back on her feet."

"But I could take her."

"You have enough on your plate right now, don't you? You're about to be mayor. Running the garage." He looked at her. "And what's going on between you and Josh?"

Shelby turned her attention back to her drink and took a long sip. "Nothing."

"It looked like something last night."

She shook her head. "I was upset over Harper, that's all. I can't date him."

"Why not?"

She couldn't believe it. Did he really not understand? "You know why not."

"Okay, he isn't the man I'd choose for you, that's for certain. He seems to be the kind of man who will get what he wants, then break your heart."

"You don't know that."

"And you do?"

Shelby shrugged. "I'm not sure."

But she was sure. Josh had grown into the type of man that even her father could admire if he was given the chance. She wouldn't say that to her father, however. She wanted to keep the peace.

"He said something interesting yesterday to me. That you might not want to win the election."

Her heart seemed to beat in her throat, so she cleared it before asking, "Why would he say something like that?"

"I was hoping that's what you would tell me." He peered at her. "Do you want to win?"

She crossed her arms over her chest. "Of course I do. I'm a Cuthbert. It's what we do."

"Is Josh right?" He stared into her eyes, and she felt as if she were four years old again and being asked if she was the one who had broken her mother's favorite figurine. "Shelby, if being mayor isn't going to make you happy, why are you running?"

"I haven't said a word, Dad. I do want to win." She did want to win. It was having to stay here as mayor that she wasn't so sure about.

"What's more important? Beating Josh or making a life you really want?"

"You're reading more into this than what's there."

"Your mother said that you haven't been happy for a while, but I thought that she was

seeing problems where there were none."
He reached over and took her hand. "Did I
force you to take over the garage?"

"No, you didn't force it on me. I agreed
that it was the right decision."

"But it's not what you would have chosen,
right? You left a good job that you loved
with that accounting firm."

"I didn't love that job. Don't fool yourself. I like being my own boss."

"But now you're keeping the garage out
of what? A sense of duty? Family honor?"
He squeezed her hand. "What do you really
want, Shelby?"

She looked down at her lap. "I don't know
anymore."

"Because of Josh?"

She looked up at him. "No. Because of
what he woke up inside me."

"What does that mean?"

She shifted in her chair to look at him
straight on. No turning. No hiding. "There's
this growing desire in me to stop playing it
safe and take a chance on something bigger
than my life here. I've been trying to drown
it out for a while now, but it won't stay quiet
anymore. And yes, Josh did that."

"So what are you going to do?"

"I promised Nana that I would always protect the family. I thought she meant keeping up the traditions on the holidays. Helping out Laurel. Buying out your business. But what if doing what's best for the family means I miss out on something that's better for me?"

"Why did you buy the garage from me if it wasn't something you wanted?"

"Because it's what you wanted. To keep it in the family. I've always known what you expect from me."

Her dad put a hand on her shoulder. "Sweetie, what I expect is for you to find what you are passionate about. What you truly want. For me, it was the garage, though it's obviously not for you."

"But what happens if I can't find it here in Thora?"

SHELBY TOSSED SOME popcorn into her mouth as the previews started in the movie theater. Next to her, Mel and Jack squabbled over who had the right to the armrest between them. Rolling her eyes, Shelby let out a soft groan. Mel turned to her. "What's wrong? Did you get a text? Is it Harper?"

Shelby gave them a pointed look. "The purpose of going to a movie tonight was to get our minds off everything going on with Harper, my sister, the election…Josh. It was to give us all a chance to relax and enjoy an evening out, right?"

Jack shrugged. "And?"

"How am I supposed to enjoy myself when you two won't stop quarreling?"

Mel placed her arm across the arm rest when Jack removed his. "We're not quarreling. We're just discussing an issue."

"Sure. And we both know that I'm right. The person to the right gets the use of the mutual armrest."

"I'm lefthanded, Jack. It's more comfortable for me to use the armrest instead of you."

Shelby eyed the pair of them. "Jack, if you put your arm around Mel's shoulders, you wouldn't have to worry about who gets to use the arm rest."

Jack's head snapped back. "Why would I put my arm around Mel? Maybe I would if the two of us were on a date, but we're not."

Mel glared at Shelby. "That's right, Shel. Jack and I are just friends."

Shelby shrugged and removed her drink from the cup holder. "Well, you could be more. Just something to think about."

Mel crossed her arms over her chest as Jack laughed at the suggestion. "I've been best friends with Mel since we were kids. Don't you think if we were going to be more than that it would have happened before now?"

"Why isn't it happening? What's wrong with you two dating?"

Mel nudged Shelby. "Drop it."

"Fine." She ate more of her popcorn and tried to focus on the previews. "Maybe the two of you should switch seats then. Mel will be on the outside and can use the arm rest there while Jack can use the one between him and I."

"Maybe you should focus on your own love life and not meddle in mine," Mel whispered before she rose to her feet and switched places with Jack.

Shelby thought about Josh. Was he home with his dad tonight? Was he getting ready for the last days before the election?

Settling into his seat, Jack leaned closer to Shelby. "Why did you say that about Mel and I dating?"

Shelby turned to look at him. "You've never wondered about what it would be like to cross that line with her?"

"She doesn't need a guy like me. I'm married to my work."

"That's a cop-out, Jack." She tipped the bag of popcorn toward him, and he took a few kernels. "You'd be lucky to have someone like Melanie."

"I know," Jack muttered as the lights went down in the theater.

Shelby rested her head against the back of the seat as the opening credits started. She was no matchmaker compared to her aunt Sarah, but she had some skill in that department. Maybe she'd planted the idea in Jack's head that would eventually flower into a relationship between her best friends.

CHAPTER ELEVEN

THE NIGHT BEFORE the election, the mayor held a town hall meeting with the candidates as a last chance to get their message out to the voters. Shelby had practiced with Mel and Jack until she felt like she could handle any question that came up. That wasn't the problem. No, her problem stood a few feet away from her going over his own notes.

Josh asked, "How's your niece?"

"Much better. Thanks. She should be released tomorrow or the day after."

He offered a warm smile. "That's great news, Shelby." He glanced out at the crowd. "You ready for this?"

"I've been ready since the day I announced my candidacy."

Josh put a hand on his belly. "I wish I could say the same. I've been popping antacids all day with the hopes of settling my stomach, but it hasn't worked yet."

She smiled. "You'll be just fine."

He looked into her eyes. "Are you okay? You seem a little sad."

"It's nothing. Break a leg tonight."

"You too."

At the stroke of seven, the current mayor, Bill, tapped on the microphone to quiet the crowd. "Good evening and welcome to tonight's event. As you know, we'll be hearing from both of the candidates. This is their last pitch to you, so be sure to ask them the tough questions before deciding on who will be our next mayor."

He waited for the applause to die down. "Many of you have asked me if I would endorse one of the candidates, and I've always said what I'm about to say now. Either of them would make a wonderful mayor for Thora. They might have different approaches to solutions, but I've discovered, as I think you all will, that they have the best in mind for our town. We will be fortunate no matter who wins the election tomorrow."

More applause before the mayor held up a hand for silence. "Without further ado, we will hear brief statements and open the floor to questions."

Shelby grinned, looking across the stage at Josh, who returned her grin. She spoke first, and then it was Josh's turn. Soon, the questions from the audience started coming. When would the new factory be opening? How many jobs were expected to be available? Josh handled those with grace and skill. Shelby could see the passion that he would bring to the office, something that wasn't always evident in the current mayor, who sometimes seemed more concerned about his interests, rather than the town's.

"Will there be an investigation of the former chief of police and his influence over his officers to drop charges?" Shelby recognized the woman who'd asked the question—Mrs. Myers from the book club that met at Melanie's bookstore.

Josh started to protest, but Shelby quickly interjected. "I'll take this one." She made eye contact with Mrs. Myers. "My uncle served Thora with distinction and honor for almost twenty years as a police officer and chief. And in all that time he was never accused of any wrongdoing. That should tell you something. That should count for something. He has explained that he had nothing to do with the charges being dropped, and I, for one, believe him and I ask that you do too, Mrs. Myers. All of you. My uncle and I would ask that the officer who claims that he was pressured in the case to come forward so that the matter can be thoroughly and fairly examined. I think we all deserve to find out what really happened that night."

A voice shouted out, "But the Cuthbert family has always controlled the story, haven't they? How can we trust that you won't change the facts to protect them?"

Shelby should have expected this. Josh came to the edge of the stage. "Tim, this is not the time."

Josh's former campaign manager scowled up at the stage. "I'd say it's about time for the citizens to throw off the Cuthbert influence."

"This election isn't about the Cuthberts," replied Shelby. "This is about discovering what's best for Thora."

"Well, it's definitely not you," Tim said before he left the meeting room.

Josh put an arm around Shelby's shoulders for a moment. "I'm sorry I ever got involved with him."

She gave him a quick nod and addressed the audience again. "I meant what I said before, folks. This election is about what's best for Thora. You need to choose the candidate who represents what you want for your future. There is a lot that my opponent and I disagree on, but we have found common ground on many issues too. Small businesses are a backbone of our community, but Josh is right. We need a diverse approach to boost Thora's bottom line. If that's the new factory, then I support it. If it's looking at other business opportunities to bring to our town, then I support that, as well."

"Sounds like you're putting your support behind Josh."

She missed who the speaker was but turned to study Josh. "Josh has proven himself to be a trustworthy man who has the interests of Thora at heart. And I would vote for him." Then she turned back to the audience and smiled. "If I wasn't running myself, that is."

A little laughter lightened the mood, and

Shelby was grateful. Josh covered the microphone and told her, "You didn't have to say that."

She simply shrugged. "It's the truth."

He swallowed, and his gaze dropped to her mouth. But he didn't kiss her. She wasn't sure if she would have responded to him if he had. Not in front of an audience. Instead, he took the next question that was asked.

JOSH TRIED TO understand why Shelby had basically handed the election to him. She may not have quit her campaign, but by endorsing him in front of all these voters, she had done the next best thing. As more questions were asked, he gave the answers he'd been practicing, but his heart was focused on the woman standing next to him.

She did love him. He knew it, but not until that instant had he believed it. She might still resist being with him, but her support meant a great deal. Maybe in time, she'd be able to ease away from the expectations of her family and pursue a relationship with him. And he realized that he'd wait as long as she needed.

The questions started to wind down, and the mayor gave his closing remarks before ending the meeting. Bill thanked them both, then exited the stage. Josh looked for Shelby, she had already joined a group of people at the back of the room. He watched her as she listened to what an older woman was telling her, nodding and making comments that he couldn't hear. She would make a great mayor. As fine a mayor as he'd ever be, maybe even better.

His dad walked over to him and patted him on the shoulder. "You did good up there."

Josh thanked him. "I wasn't as poised as Shelby though. She was something, wasn't she?"

His dad peered at him. "You really do like her."

Josh winced. "No, I'm in love with her."

His dad whistled and scratched the top of his head. "That's a real predicament, isn't it? How does she feel about that?"

"You heard what she said up there."

"So, what are you going to do about it?"

"Nothing, Dad. She's made it clear that she's sticking by her family and that includes what they think about me. And about anything else."

"Maybe it's like Tim said, then. It's time for the influence of the Cuthberts to end. Even from Shelby's shoulders." His father looked to where Shelby still stood talking to the group of older women. "I wouldn't let that get in your way regardless. And it never seemed to bother you before."

"What would Joe have done?"

"Doesn't matter. This is your life. Go after her, since it's what you really want."

"I will after the election."

"I wouldn't wait that long."

Josh squeezed his dad's shoulder affectionately before approaching Shelby. He waited while she made promises to get back with the women's group about a future community project, mayor or not. She caught sight of him. "You were wonderful tonight," she said.

He glanced at the crowd, which was still socializing. "Can we go talk somewhere? Just the two of us?"

"I don't think that's a good idea."

"The election is tomorrow, and I have

things I want to say to you before this all ends. Please, Shelby."

"Tomorrow's a long day for the both of us. Let's just say good-night here, and we can talk later."

"Are you afraid of being alone with me?"

"That's silly." Shelby's gaze told him she was doubtful. "There's nothing else left to say."

"There's plenty to be said between us."

Shelby gestured at a couple that kept looking over at them. "Don't do this here."

"If you won't go somewhere else with me, I have no choice." He took a deep breath. "I'm in love with you, and I want to be with you. And it doesn't matter what the voters or anyone else thinks. We should be together. Come on, Shelby, don't you feel that too?"

"Josh, you don't mean—"

"I've meant every word that I've said to you. And none of this will be worth anything if I don't have you by my side." Shelby stared at him, and he held out his hand to her. "Please tell me that you want me too."

She looked at his hand, then up into his eyes and slowly shook her head. "I can't."

ELECTION MORNING ON that August day started with a scorching heat. Shelby dressed in the most summery and patriotic outfit she had: a navy blue sleeveless dress with red and white stars. She carefully put her hair up in a neat bun that would keep it off her neck in this humid weather, since she planned on visiting local businesses to shake hands and talk to voters.

When she arrived at her first stop, the community center where she was registered to vote, she found that Aunt Sarah had brought a contingent of seniors from the home, including Mr. Duffy who sat in his wheelchair beside her. She looked from one to the other, and her great-aunt actually blushed before shrugging. Well, well. That was an interesting development.

Shelby went inside the building to vote. In the booth, she paused as she stared at her name above Josh's, the pen poised where she would mark her choice. Common sense told her to mark her own name, but the urge to choose Josh's made her pause.

Her or Josh? She looked back down at the ballot before closing her eyes. What did she want the most? She debated internally for

several moments before making her mark
and striding out of the booth with her ballot
inside the privacy envelope. She handed it
to Mr. Hooks, who was working at the polling station that morning, smiled at him and
went to join the group outside.

Shelby took her place with her aunt's con-
tingency and greeted voters as they arrived.
She glanced at Aunt Sarah. "So you and Mr.
Duffy are back on, then?"

Her aunt beamed and looked over to
where he was talking to Link, the caretaker
for the town hall as well as the schools when
they were in session. "I've discovered that a
love like ours isn't on or off. It simply is."

Shelby hugged her aunt. "You deserve all
this happiness and more."

"That's kind, Shelby. I hope you'll find
your own happiness one day."

"I've certainly found mine," Mr. Duffy
said as he wheeled up to them. "Dumpling,
aren't you happy with me?"

Aunt Sarah reached down and pulled him
into a kiss that made Shelby blush. "Ec-
static."

Mr. Duffy cleared his throat and looked

at Shelby. "I hope you don't mind if I join your family gatherings in the future."

"I insist on it. In fact, if she can't bring you, I'll come and get you myself."

Mr. Duffy tipped his head back and laughed. "My Sarah said that you had a knack for leadership. That's why I voted for you this morning."

"Me too," her aunt chimed in.

Shelby felt gratified. "Thank you both. I appreciate the support." She noticed the constant stream of early voters entering and leaving the building. "How has the turnout been so far?"

"Above average, I'd say. Many people are mentioning they've voted for you, so I don't know how effective Tim's behavior has been. Thankfully." Aunt Sarah had worked the polls in years past, so her words had authority. "Things look favorable for you right now."

"I should have hired you for my team."

"My organizing days are over. Which reminds me that we need to discuss my replacement for the family's annual Christmas fundraiser. December will be here before you know it."

"I can't do it without you, Aunt Sarah. I only worked on last year's, and there's still so much you have to teach me."

Aunt Sarah put her hand on Mr. Duffy's shoulder. "Well, Henry and I are planning on getting married on New Year's Eve, so you and I will have to figure something out."

Shelby's mouth dropped open as she looked at her aunt first, then her intended, who smiled widely at his fiancée. "Are you serious?" Shelby asked.

"We don't want to miss another minute together, so we figured that we should do it soon."

Shelby grabbed her great-aunt and hugged her, closing her eyes at the emotions that threatened to fall as tears. "This is unbelievable." When she let go of her aunt, she embraced Henry just as tightly. "Congratulations. You're getting an amazing woman."

"Took me long enough to swallow my pride and admit what was right in front of me."

Shelby smiled at the two of them. "Have you told the family?"

They shared a look before Aunt Sarah said, "Not exactly. And you are sworn to secrecy. With Penny and Christopher's wedding later this month, we thought we'd wait until after to share the news. Don't want to steal their big moment."

"Steal? This would make it even better."

"I told Penny since she'll be my matron of honor and now you. But that's it. The news goes no further, understand?"

Shelby nodded and clapped her hands. "I can't wait to start planning."

"That's the thing, dear. Henry and I will arrange everything. All we need you to do is show up on the day."

"Perhaps with him as your date?" Henry asked.

"Who?" Shelby spotted Josh standing not far from them. He held up his hand in greeting, and she acknowledged him, keeping her eyes on him. "No. I'm not dating Josh."

"The election is today," Aunt Sarah said with enthusiasm. "Whatever the result, you're free now to do what you want."

"I never said being with Josh is what I wanted."

"The look on your face says otherwise."

JOSH KNEW THAT he'd run into Shelby today, but he hadn't expected it to be so early. His dad nudged his arm. "Are we going in to vote or what?"

Josh swallowed and said, "Sorry, I was distracted."

His dad grinned. "I know what distracted you. Did you ever talk to her about a future?"

"Yes. And she doesn't want me, Dad."

"I'd say that was up for debate. Look at her. She can't take her eyes off you." His dad cleared his throat and started to walk faster. "Think I'll go wish her luck."

"Dad…" He groaned and hurried to catch up to his father.

Shelby didn't smile as they approached but neither did she look away. "We wanted to wish you good luck," Josh said.

She gave a nod. "You too."

They stood gazing at each other, wordlessly. His dad started to chuckle. "Think I'll go cast my vote. Best of luck, Shelby."

She didn't seem to register that his dad had spoken. Instead, she took a step toward him and said, "Today will decide a lot of things. For the both of us."

"I've already made my decision. I can do good things for Thora without being mayor.

I just want to be with you, Shelby, if you can meet me halfway. I don't care how the election turns out anymore."

"You can't mean that."

"It's the truth." He took a hold of her bare upper arms. "You're what's important. Us, or what could be us…"

Shelby bit her lip and stepped back. Did she want to say yes, to finally take that leap she'd never been able to before? Out of the corner of his eye, he saw her aunt and Henry, and how sweet and joyful they were in each other's company. Couldn't she see that she could have that too, if only she believed in what they had?

"I'm sure I'll be running into you at the other polling locations. Good luck, Josh." She hurried off.

"That woman is so stubborn," he murmured.

"She's finding herself, Josh. Give her time. She'll see the truth." Aunt Sarah put a hand on his arm. "Sometimes it's hard to go against what others expect from you."

"I hope so." He wasn't sure how much more his heart could take.

JOSH HELD HIS postelection party at the bar his dad had once frequented. He'd invited friends of his father, volunteers who had passed out literature and answered phones, and anyone else he could think of. Even Mr. Hooks had promised to stop by once the ballots were counted.

Josh glanced at his watch. Only a few more minutes for the last few voters to get their voices heard. Had he done enough to win?

And would it matter, if he didn't have Shelby?

He sighed and took a sip of his beer, staring at the television that played at the corner of the bar. His cell buzzed, and he glanced at the caller ID. Probably a reporter. Disappointed that it wasn't Shelby trying to talk to him, he stuffed the phone back into his pocket.

His dad turned on his bar stool to look at him. "You're not going to take that?"

"No one I want to talk to right now."

"Ah." His dad went back to watching the baseball game. "You could call her first, you know."

"She's made her position very clear. I don't have a chance."

"Well, I'm sure sorry to hear that because, son, I've learned a lot about you in the past months you've lived with me. And even more in the last couple of weeks when you didn't. And shame on me for not saying it sooner." His dad put a hand on his shoulder. "You're a good man. And I'm proud to call you my son."

Josh stared at his father. Words he'd longed to hear his whole life still rang in the air as he tried to blink back tears. "I am?" He barely got out the last syllable, his voice soft and low.

His dad nodded. "Your brother couldn't have done any better."

Josh pulled his dad into his arms, tightening the hug. The old man patted him a couple of times, but Josh couldn't let him go. "Thank you for saying that."

"It's just too bad your mother didn't live long enough to see this."

Both men let go, blinking their eyes and clearing their throats of the whirl of emotion they'd stirred up for themselves. His dad turned back to his drink, and Josh did the same.

The election results could go his way or not. He'd gotten one of the things that he'd wanted most. Now he had to figure out how to get the other.

THE RESULTS PARTY for Shelby's campaign was held at the same rental hall the family used for most of their community social events. Melanie had decorated the room with red and blue balloons and hired a caterer who served finger foods and two-bite desserts. Shelby picked at the mini corn dog as her mother asked her, "Any word?"

The polls had closed almost an hour ago, but her phone had remained silent. She'd heard nothing about the outcome. This was it. The next hour or so would determine her future. Either she'd be mayor and lose Josh or she'd lose both. Didn't seem like much of a choice since she wouldn't have what she really wanted, no matter what happened.

She should have taken his hand this morning. Should have told him that she wanted him just as much. But she'd been a coward. Afraid those things like family and the election would keep them apart. But what scared her most was that she'd be like Aunt Sarah, waiting more than fifty years until she could finally be with her beloved.

She shook her head. "Any word from Laurel?"

"Your dad said that she can't have any visitors at the rehab center until she reaches the thirty-day mark. But she thinks that this time it will work."

"And Harper?"

"Uncle Rick and Aunt June are at the hospital covering for us now. The doctors should be releasing Harper tomorrow morning. Your dad and I will go get her."

"If you need me to watch her…"

Her mom put a hand on her shoulder. "You've done enough for them, Shelby. Besides, once you're mayor you won't have the time to take care of her and the business on top of everything else."

"It's no problem."

Her mother kissed her cheek. "You don't have to take everything on. It's okay to let others do things too."

"And what if I decide to do something you don't like?"

"Such as?"

"Never mind. Forget I said anything."

Melanie approached her with a glass of champagne and thrust it into one of her empty hands. "Let's celebrate early."

"We don't know if I won yet."

"But you will." Melanie took a sip of her drink and watched Shelby over the rim of the glass. "For someone about to be mayor, you don't seem very happy."

"I haven't won."

"Almost."

"I can't pin all my hopes on an almost." She glanced around the room, longing to leave her own party. "I gotta go." She turned and walked away, putting the champagne glass down at an empty table.

Melanie followed her. "Where are you going?"

"I don't know. I just need to get out of here. I need some space to think." She hugged Melanie and tried to smile. "I appreciate all the work you did to get me elected, but I need some time alone now."

"What if they call you with the results?"

"I'll let you know as soon as I do."

She practically ran out of the venue and headed for her Mustang, but realized she'd left her purse with the keys inside the building. She couldn't go back in or she would change her mind and stay. She could walk to city hall, so she set off in that direction. Maybe she could find out the results sooner. But once she reached the park next to it, she realized that she didn't want to wait around there either, because win or lose, she had a choice she was going to have to make.

She took a seat on one of the swings and let her legs dangle. Her cell phone rang, and she looked at the display. Josh. She answered it and placed it to her ear. "Have you heard anything?"

"No. You?"

"No."

She listened to him breathing on the other end. She knew she should end the call. The clerk's office might be trying to get a hold of her. She cleared her throat. "I'll call you if I hear."

"I need to see you."

"Why?" Being with him would only confuse her more. She needed to think about what she was going to do after this election, mayor or not. Her life had to change, but she was still figuring out the details of how that would look.

"I know we can make this work, Shelby. We love each other, so we can figure it out."

She closed her eyes and tried to swallow the lump in her throat. "We decided this already. There's nothing to figure out."

"What about wanting to be with me as much as I want to be with you, election or not?"

"I can't be with you."

"Because you don't want me? Or because you're too afraid to go after something that you really want that your family and friends might not approve of?"

Oh, how she wanted him. Wanted him just as he was and for who he was. To spend every day with him beside her. To see where the future could take them, as long as they were together. But she couldn't say any of that. Wouldn't say it.

"I need to see you," he said. "Where are you?"

"It's not going to change anything, so what's the point?"

"I want to hear the election results with you by my side. Is that too much to ask?"

She debated whether to tell him her location or not. But he was right. They should hear the results together. "Meet me at the park, by the swings."

"I'll be right there."

She hung up and wondered what she'd say to him once he arrived. She texted Melanie to let her know that she hadn't heard anything yet but would call soon after she did. Texted her mom to say the same thing, then put the phone back into her pocket. She placed her hands on the chains of the swing and stood before pushing off, letting the momentum take her a little higher with each pump of her legs.

She had an opportunity to find her own happiness, so why did she feel as if she was about to throw it away? To tamp down her desire for Josh and a life with him in order to keep the family peace. To keep doing what she always had. Put everyone else and their feelings ahead of her own. She'd always done that.

But what if she seized this chance? Hadn't she lectured Mel about telling Jack her feelings and taking the risk on being with him? And yet she was about to do the exact opposite. To tell Josh that there could be no future for them.

Shelby closed her eyes as the swing slowed to a stop. It was like planning a trip to Greece that she'd never take all over again. She couldn't go and leave her family because they needed her. But what about what she needed? Didn't she deserve to lie on a white sand beach near a turquoise sea with a drink in her hand and not a worry in her head?

And didn't she also deserve that chance with Josh? Her heart said yes, but her mind reminded her of all the reasons she couldn't.

Her cell phone rang, and she glanced at the caller ID. It was the city clerk. She took a deep breath, then answered it. She smiled when she heard the results.

JOSH LEFT HIS truck curbside next to the park. His cell phone buzzed again, but he didn't care. The only thing that mattered was to get to Shelby. She was wrong about them. They could work it out. He believed in her, and he hoped she could believe in him. Together, they could believe in their future with each other.

He crested the hill and saw her sitting on a swing, turning it in circles, raising her feet so that she tilted back, her hair flowing behind her. He smiled and strode the last few steps toward her. She looked up at him, and he wished he could bend down to kiss her upturned mouth.

He took a seat on the swing next to her and glanced at her. She slowed and turned to look at him. "The city clerk called me."

He noted the satisfied smile on her face and pushed aside his disappointment. "Congratulations, Shelby. I know you'll make a fantastic mayor."

She beamed at him. "That's just it. It was really close, but I didn't win."

He got off his swing and grabbed both chains of hers to keep her from moving. "What did you say?"

She hopped to her feet and looked into his eyes. "The congratulations go to you, Mr. Mayor. And you're going to be amazing. I just know it."

He took a step away from her. Shaking his head, he said, "I'm so sorry."

"Don't be. I'm not." She stepped toward him and put her hands on either side of his face. "Honestly, I'm pretty relieved. You were right. I was running for mayor of a town I want to leave. But to go exploring the big wide world out there. And if I'd won, I'd have to be here instead for the next four years."

He put his hands on hers and asked, "So what are you going to do now?"

"That's the big question, isn't it? I've been evaluating my life lately. Figuring out what I want, outside of my family's expectations."

His breath seemed to catch in his chest. "What do you want, Shelby?" *Please say me.*

"It's easier for me to say what I don't want." Suddenly, it was as if she had taken a piece of his heart and was about to run. "I don't want to own the garage. It might break my father's heart when I tell him, but I bet Eddie is interested in buying the business from me." She looked away from him. "And I don't want to spend another year planning a trip that I never go on."

"But, Shelby, you didn't answer my question. What do *you* want?"

"For starters?" When he nodded, she closed the gap between them and put her arms around his waist. "To be with you. Always. Forever. Oh, and I'm booking a ticket to Athens as soon as I can. I'm thinking that a month in Greece will be a good start to figuring out the rest of my life." She smiled up at him. "Want to come with me? The way I see it, there's things we need to decide together."

He nodded, returned her smile before leaning in to kiss her. "I just need to be back in time to be sworn in as mayor."

"And I'll be right there, backing you every step of the way. I love you, Josh."

He swept her into his arms. It felt so right, she thought. "With you supporting me, there won't be anything I or we can't do. I love you too, Shelby."

HOLDING JOSH'S HAND, Shelby entered the hall where her post-election party was being held and scanned the crowd. It was time to make her concession speech and thank all the volunteers for their time and support.

She looked into Josh's eyes and smiled at him. He nodded at her, kissed her hand before releasing her. Her mother approached them, looking behind Shelby at Josh. "What is he doing here? This is your victory party. Have you heard the results?"

"Have you seen Melanie? I have an announcement to make."

Her mother beamed and put her hands on her arms. "Congratulations, sweetheart. We knew you could do it."

Shelby stepped back. "Not that kind of announcement, Mom."

She walked past her mother and found Melanie chatting with Jack. "I've heard from the clerk's office. Do you think you could get a microphone so I can address the crowd, Jack?"

"On it," Jack said and left the two women.

Melanie glanced over at Josh. "That's awfully big of him. To make an appearance at your victory party. I'm kind of surprised he'd show up here."

"He's going to be a bigger part of my life after this. Why shouldn't he be here now?"

Jack had a microphone ready for her within seconds, and Shelby made a motion to Melanie to cut the music. When the tunes stopped, she gripped the microphone tightly in her hand. She was ready. This was what she truly wanted. "Thank you one and all for your hard work during this campaign. We made a strong effort to get me elected, but the voters have spoken and have chosen Josh Riley instead as our next mayor."

Boos sounded from around the room, but Shelby shook her head. "No, this is a good night for Thora. The town has chosen an honorable man who believes in Thora and what we can achieve together. And I plan on supporting Josh every step of the way." She looked over and smiled at him. "I hope that you all will fall in love with him just as I have." She reached out her hand to him, and he joined her, clasping her hand in his.

She turned from Josh to the crowd. Many of her family members were there, but also friends and so many others who had volunteered for her campaign. They had worked so hard for her to succeed and she would make her success theirs. "The last few months have shown me what is possible here in Thora. I can't wait to get started. The future is full of possibilities. It's going to take all of us working as a team to make that future a reality for this town. With Josh at the helm, I believe it will happen. Ladies and gentlemen, I'd like you to meet your next mayor, Josh Riley."

She promptly handed the microphone to Josh. He waved to the crowd, gave Shelby a quick hug, smiling. "I hope to be worthy of your support, Shelby. Now and always. And I promise to do my best for Thora. Thank you, everyone."

He turned off the microphone and handed it to Jack who was staring at her and Josh. Her mother came forward and Shelby put her hand into Josh's, waiting for her mother's censure. She'd always done what was expected, but this was her turn to do what was right for herself. Josh was good for her. They believed in each other. Nana might have asked her to always protect the family, but she'd never said that Shelby had to sacrifice her own desires to achieve that.

Josh squeezed her hand as her mother eyed him from head to toe. Finally, she sighed and pointed at Josh. "You don't deserve her."

"I know, ma'am. But I hope to spend the rest of my life trying to prove myself."

Her mother faced her. "I can't say that I'm happy about this, but…" She gave a soft smile. "I only want you to be happy."

"I will be."

"So, what will you do now that the election is over?"

Shelby grinned at Josh. "I'm going to travel for a while. And then decide the rest of my life in the new year."

Her mom nodded and went to join her dad. But Shelby wasn't really aware of anything else. She was focused only on the man standing next to her. "So, what should we do with the rest of our lives?" she asked him.

"I vote that we take life as it comes."

"As long as we do it together, right?"

"Together. My favorite place to be in the whole wide world." He pulled her close and kissed her.

* * * * *

For more great romances from
Syndi Powell and
Harlequin Heartwarming,
visit www.Harlequin.com today!

Get 4 FREE REWARDS!

We'll send you 2 FREE Books <u>plus</u> 2 FREE Mystery Gifts.

Love Inspired Suspense books showcase how courage and optimism unite in stories of faith and love in the face of danger.

FREE Value Over **$20**

YES! Please send me 2 FREE Love Inspired Suspense novels and my 2 FREE mystery gifts (gifts are worth about $10 retail). After receiving them, if I don't wish to receive any more books, I can return the shipping statement marked "cancel." If I don't cancel, I will receive 6 brand-new novels every month and be billed just $5.24 each for the regular-print edition or $5.99 each for the larger-print edition in the U.S., or $5.74 each for the regular-print edition or $6.24 each for the larger-print edition in Canada. That's a savings of at least 13% off the cover price. It's quite a bargain! Shipping and handling is just 50¢ per book in the U.S. and $1.25 per book in Canada.* I understand that accepting the 2 free books and gifts places me under no obligation to buy anything. I can always return a shipment and cancel at any time. The free books and gifts are mine to keep no matter what I decide.

Choose one: ☐ **Love Inspired Suspense Regular-Print** (153/353 IDN GNWN) ☐ **Love Inspired Suspense Larger-Print** (107/307 IDN GNWN)

Name (please print)

Address   Apt. #

City   State/Province   Zip/Postal Code

Email: Please check this box ☐ if you would like to receive newsletters and promotional emails from Harlequin Enterprises ULC and its affiliates. You can unsubscribe anytime.

Mail to the **Harlequin Reader Service:**
IN U.S.A.: P.O. Box 1341, Buffalo, NY 14240-8531
IN CANADA: P.O. Box 603, Fort Erie, Ontario L2A 5X3

Want to try 2 free books from another series? Call 1-800-873-8635 or visit www.ReaderService.com.

Visit
ReaderService.com
Today!

As a valued member of the Harlequin Reader Service, you'll find these benefits and more at ReaderService.com:

- Try 2 free books from any series
- Access risk-free special offers
- View your account history & manage payments
- Browse the latest Bonus Bucks catalog

Don't miss out!

If you want to stay up-to-date on the latest at the Harlequin Reader Service and enjoy more content, make sure you've signed up for our monthly News & Notes email newsletter. Sign up online at ReaderService.com or by calling Customer Service at 1-800-873-8635.

RS20